There Is No Borges

There Is No Borges

a novel
Gerhard Köpf

Translated by Leslie Willson

George Braziller
New York

First published in the United States of America in 1993
by George Braziller, Inc.

English translation copyright © Leslie Willson
Originally published in German.

Copyright © 1992 by Luchterhand Verlag under the title
Borges gibt es nicht

All Rights Reserved.

For information, please write to the publisher:

George Braziller, Inc.
60 Madison Avenue
New York, New York
10010

Library of Congress Cataloging-in-Publication Data

Köpf, Gerhard, 1948–
    [Borges gibt es nicht. English]
    There is no Borges / Gerhard Köpf
      p.   cm.
    ISBN 0-8076-1323-6 : $18.50
    I. Title.
PT2671.0548B613   1993   93-482
833'.914—dc20   CIP

Printed and bound in the United States of America

First U.S. edition 1993

There Is No
Borges

We neither say
who we were,
nor describe our life
the way we lived it,
rather we will live it
the way we tell it.

John Edward Lovelock

1

Atmospheric High

There was a smell of snow in the air, my love life was a mess, my work had become a mockery, my parents had died, my friends had turned away from me.

I was at the end of my rope. I locked the doors and windows and became absorbed so deeply in the world of books that my nights from twilight to dawn and my days from dawn to dusk passed while I was reading.

Only books remained.

Then the invitation to make this lecture tour caught me by surprise. At first I thought it was a cruel joke by my adversaries to humiliate me further, but then I was repeatedly assured that I was the one they wanted, explicitly and in all seriousness.

Apparently it hadn't reached the farthest corners

of the world that I was finished. Or it may be that my sponsors weren't concerned by the voices that had publicly and emphatically confirmed that I had hit bottom.

I couldn't help marveling mistrustfully at the courage of those who wanted to pay me for this tour. It could be only a kind of supra-courage that had beguiled them.

So I accepted gratefully, left my tower, stepped into the aluminum belly of a long-distance plane, buckled my seat belt, and flew, as I was naive enough to believe, toward the sun, as though an unexpected vacation trip were involved.

To fly eastward means to outwit time and play a trick on it. Any child knows that. You pay for it only after landing, when you always get tired at the wrong time and are wide awake at the wrong time. Your whole organism gets unsettled. Airplanes are nothing more than machines for the destruction of time and distance.

Nothing makes sense anymore at this altitude.

Everything is suspended.

Only anxieties and longings drive you from place to place and give you no peace.

Why in the world Surabaya, why in the world one of the most wretched cities you can imagine?

Because of Jonny?

No. Because of *Almayer's Folly*.

When had I read that novel for the first time?

It was definitely a Thursday. It must have been a Thursday. There's something about my Thursdays.

On a Thursday I left Surabaya.

Actually, before the flight I wanted to get the recipe for the flying underpants that had tasted so good to me: a handkerchief-sized, rolled-out pastry that was tossed into boiling fat with an operatic gesture by the cook, furbished with a filling of some kind of ground meat, and finally served folded up like underpants.

But I had been unable to do it for lack of time. What lured me to Surabaya was the cemetery, a very specific cemetery. When I had finally found it, the cemetery attendant drew me aside, offered me one of his aromatic cigarettes. "*Rokok Kretik*," he said, "*andang garam*," which means sweat glands; he tugged at the hairs on my arms, fumbled at my face, pulled at my beard, testing whether it was real, and asked finally in a conspiratorial tone whether I had come because of Hitler.

Why Hitler?

Hitler was buried here, everyone in Surabaya knew that: fled from Germany on a submarine and buried here. In this cemetery. There was proof.

But I hadn't come for that reason. I had been harried here by a few sentences I had once read that afterward gave me no peace. I had taken on all the hardships of this detour from my itinerary because of a book. Heat and nearly unbearable humidity, so that my glasses fogged up as soon as I left air-conditioned hotel rooms. Even after two minutes everything stuck to my body; horrible streets, dilapidated overnight lodgings, cramped taxis with tattered seats and expectorating drivers. And again and again hands that fumble around on my face and can't get enough of tugging and jerking.

I had come because of a Dutchman named Olmayer, who I knew lay buried in Surabaya. Not even the artfully garrulous cemetery attendant knew exactly where. What I knew about Olmayer I had read in Joseph Conrad. More than a hundred years ago the Pole, forced by a tropical fever to give up his vocation as a sailor, had written his first novel about him.

Almayer's Folly tells the desperate tale of the Dutch merchant Olmayer. A true story, so it was called.

Ever since I read the book, I had wanted to go to Surabaya, for in Almayer I recognized one of us: *He absorbed himself in his dream of wealth and power away from this coast where he had dwelt for so many years, forgetting the bitterness of toil and strife in the vision of a great and splendid reward.*

And that was not supposed to be one of us? Do not we, too, absorb ourselves in dreams of wealth and power, do not we, too, each on his own, find ourselves on a coast where we don't belong, do not we, too, long for a splendid reward, even if it be on a day howsoever far away?

They would live in Europe, he and his daughter. They would be rich and respected.... Witnessing her triumphs he would grow young again, he would forget the twenty-five years of heartbreaking struggle on this coast where he felt like a prisoner.

Already I see the lovely Nina before me:...a woman, black-haired, olive-skinned, tall, and beautiful, with great sad eyes, where the startled expression common to Malay womankind was modified by a thoughtful tinge inherited from her European ancestry.

That's how Joseph Conrad saw her, and he tells us the tale of a foundering dreamer, about whom he says: Good fortune seemed to escape his grasp again and again.

When I was looking for the grave at the cemetery, everything was exactly as Conrad had described it, and it seemed to me as though I had experienced all of this, as though I were leafing only in my memories and not in a book.

I have always taken actuality from books and then considered anything of reality that then was added as a staging idea, which might have to do with the production of the play but not with the play itself. I have always moved through the world reading, because for me nothing is more precise than fiction. I have explained my life and the world with books and have never been disappointed in doing so. Knowledge from books is not secondhand as they like to declare, rather supposed reality is secondhand for me. What was in books has always fitted to a T.

Even the moon mounted higher, and the warm shadows grew smaller and crept away.

I was alone with Almayer. Conrad describes him as one who wonders whether he was to be tormented through all eternity, as one of us insomniacs who can find their peace neither in daytime nor at night. In the cemetery of Surabaya I heard his monotonous whisper, *like an instrument, all the strings but one of which had snapped under a violent thrum.* I saw him move through his house, and in anxiety and hurt wait for that oblivion that appeared so hesitantly—for that oblivion from which we hope for redemption. After his idolized daughter had left him, Almayer wanted nothing more than to live only long enough to be able to forget. *And the stubbornness of his memories filled him with the fear and dread of death.*

Such phrases drove me at night to the cemetery of Surabaya.

That can be fully understood only by someone who would rather read his life than have to live it from defeat to defeat, tiresomely and evasively.

With the sentences of Conrad in mind I drove to the airport, surrendered my luggage, and waited until the passengers were called for Bandung and were carted to their plane in a pitiable bus with plate-sized rust holes in its floor, past airplanes at the edge of the runway ready for junk: like cattle to the slaughterhouse.

A GARUDA Fokker Friendship was waiting for us.

No, the word did not refer to the mythical bird that hangs on walls, carved from wood, with its mouth open ravenously, an old man had informed me in the waiting room. GARUDA was the abbreviation for *good airline ruled under Dutch administration*, just as the Portuguese TAP means nothing more than *take another plane*, the Belgian SABENA *such a bad experience never again*, the British BOAC *better on a camel*, the Japanese JAL *just a lie*.... And the old man revealed his gold tooth while laughing.

Coincidence or providence: The old man took a seat next to me at the window, forced his girth onto the narrow cushions while I buckled myself into the seat on the aisle, from which I had a good view into the cockpit. Our captain couldn't have been thirty years old. He loosened his tie, unbuttoned his shirt wide, lighted a cigarette—and turned on the No Smoking sign. And he was wearing high-topped boxing shoes with cutout heels, tied above his ankles: like waitresses in train station restaurants, whom I have always studied observantly.

I pulled *Almayer's Folly* out of my pocket and was about to reread a few passages when my neighbor tugged at my sleeve, his eyes fastened on my book, and remarked that Conrad was a decent writer, even Borges admitted it. Conrad was even *the* novelist for him, but, compared with Borges, Conrad was, in the final analysis, no more than an orphan boy.

I don't like persons who always have to play one off against another. I never have understood their zeal, nor the satisfaction they get from that kind of silly comparison.

The old man must have noticed my discontent, for he began to appease me in a conciliatory tone, and I couldn't avoid letting myself be drawn into a conversation with him:

"To reach death there is no faster vehicle than habit, sweet monotony. But if you want to enjoy life and memories, travel!"

He talked unswervingly about travel and finally was of the opinion that existence was travel enough, even if the shortest way to one's own Self presumably led around the world. Only the most unconscionable weakness of the imagination justified that you had only to change your place to feel: Every road bears you to the end of the world. But the end of the world, as soon as you have completely circled the globe, is the same duck puddle from which you started out: our conception of the world. Only in ourselves were landscapes a landscape; therefore the traveler created them by imagining them. If he created them, then they existed. If they existed, he looked at them as did others. So why travel? Life was what we made of it. Travel was the travelers. What we saw wasn't what we saw but what we were.

Did those kinds of pompous considerations come from Borges? This was what I wanted to know from the old man.

"No," he replied, those thoughts were by a man who had taken shelter his whole life behind other names. Of course, they had put up a memorial for him in a monastery fifty years after his death, but to this day no one knew his real name. By the way, that could apply equally well to Borges.

My interjection was received with a mild smile. In the case of Borges, I said, the matter was completely unambiguous, everyone knew who Borges was.

The plane began to roar and to tremble and, to my great astonishment, finally moved off with sluggish jolts. The door had not yet been closed; apparently it was stuck. Two flight attendants were struggling with all their might, with blowing skirts, to wrench the handle around. The open door didn't seem to bother our captain. He was already steering the plane to the takeoff position, already pushing the fuel lever forward—and the door was still not closed. The Fokker gathered speed, rolled faster and faster, but the door remained open. The stewardesses pulled and tugged, their skirts billowed and fluttered, the door wouldn't close. We took off from Surabaya with an open door. A strong windstream gripped the cabin. That didn't seem to make my neighbor at all uneasy, for he calmly asked me whether I had enjoyed the famous flying underpants in Surabaya: a delicacy.... But what did I care about flying underpants at a moment when the draft had completely gripped the cabin, inflated shirts and blouses, tore at pants legs, and made hair stand straight up. Finally it pushed even into the cockpit, where the captain, a cigarette in his mouth, pulled the control column toward him and sawed our Fokker into the sky.

At last the two slim girls succeeded in turning the handle around and closing the door.

My gaze had fastened onto the heels of the captain. The smoking sign was on.

"GARUDA," said my neighbor, "good airline.... Permit me, my name is *Christofari*."

I felt dizzy and fuzzy-headed while the old man kept on talking and, after God and the world, got around to Borges again. One word led to another, and slowly I recovered from the fright that the takeoff with an open door had given me. The old man wandered from one thing to another, got lost in details, until finally he got me to the point where he inveigled my memories out of me.

When the death of the poet Borges was announced to a world no longer subject to surprise, I just happened to be in Rome. I was on my way to a movie. Disgusted by the crowding and shoving I had left the overcrowded bus at Barberini, had strolled down the Tritone, and had bought myself some newspapers that, as I walked on the Corso in the direction of the Piazza Venezia, I was scanning. The evening sun dipped the Altar of the Fatherland into an unreal light, and that architectural piece of vomit reared like a gigantic typewriter into the Roman sky. For a moment I remained standing on the sidewalk and read the headlines, which said: BORGES IL MINOTAURO MALINCONICO! IL GRANDE SCRITTORE ARGENTINO E MORTO IERI A GINEVRA ALL' ETA DI OTTANTASEI ANNI.

Next to them and under them were articles by Carmelo Samoná and Antonio Tabbuchi as well as photographs of an old man who, propped by a cane, was sitting in an armchair fit for a pope or a dictator.

Borges was smiling his mischievous reptilian smile. The hands gripping the cane once gently touched the pages of the *Edda* in Reykjavík, a privilege that in our century was extended only to the young queen of Sweden.

I noticed something else in the paper: between semi-bold and bold the photograph of a very slender woman with careworn features—

Maria Kodama, the wife of Jorge Luis Borges for only a short time. A widow with thin lips.

At the end of October in 1982 I met Borges personally in the Munich Academy of Fine Arts. I even got him to sign a book: *Unicorn, Sphinx, and Salamander. The Book of Imaginary Creatures*. Borges himself seemed an imaginary creature to me; and had not the official speaker ended his address with the thought that Borges, in the final analysis, may have been nothing more than an invention of Borges?

I gladly admit that, more than all the clever essays, more than the obscure poems and the many-layered, intricate, shrewdly interwoven stories that alluded to God and the world of literature and philosophy, more than all the labyrinths and black mirrors, and every page of the Library of Babel, more than the entire work of this mythical figure, I was above all always fascinated by one particular: The blind poet Borges was the director of the National Library. The mystery of the books seemed to me to be expressed in that paradox. Did this man surrounded by legend really exist, or was he only a fata morgana from Buenos Aires? But in the Academy of Fine Arts I had Borges before me in the flesh. The great Borges had signed my copy of the *Book of Imaginary Creatures*: What a brilliant scribble on the half-title page, executed with an ordinary ballpoint pen.

His name seemed to me to be a distinctive mark of recognition among initiates, admittedly saddled with the petty reproach of critics that he was still only a writer's writer.

One part from the epilogue of *Borges and Me* occurred to me, where it says: "Someone sets himself the task of copying the world. In the course of the years he populates a space with images of provinces, kingdoms, mountain ranges, bays, ships, islands, fish, habitations, tools, star clusters, horses, and persons. Shortly before he dies, he discovers that this patient labyrinth of lines reproduces the image of his own face."

Anyone who could write like that was capable of anything, in my opinion, even bringing forth the strikingly lovely story about the blind poet as a library director, in which he was gladly trapped, especially since Borges was able not only to tell the story brilliantly but also to live up to it himself.

I was immersed in that thought when I turned left at the Piazza Venezia and set my steps in the direction of the Via Quattro.

Once Borges, who was called a seer by his followers, spoke to students on the theme of growing old. At the very beginning of his lecture he was whistled down with derision. But he enjoyed it to such an extent that he dispensed with his remarks, gratefully acknowledged the friendly reception ironically, and declared himself ready to answer any and all questions. He dignified particularly stupid questions with his silence. Asked about the future, Borges answered that the future presumably did not exist. It was made up of memories of the past. We expected that what was present would become real or be contradicted. In actuality, not even he knew who he was. Therefore he had written it down a couple of times. Finally there was great applause, which had been as inconceivable as the whistling at the start. At the end Borges is said to have called out to the students: "I'm amazed that you read me. Read someone else."

What an exit line!

The plane lay quietly in the air, the motors roared evenly, the stewardesses began to serve. With the coffee was a box of candy that I opened immediately and in doing so came across a brochure with the title "Coronation of a Great Love." The thin, illustrated booklet reported the wedding of the Duke and Duchess of York: "The bride beamed, the father of the bride was near collapse. Thousands formed a lane when the wedding procession moved through the inner part of London. Many had spent the night before in sleeping bags along the street, so they could see the bride up close. It probably was the happiest wedding ever enjoyed by the Royal Family of England. Sarah and Andrew rode off delighted on their honeymoon. I will love you, serve and obey you until death do us part. The bride had insisted specifically on the old refrain. Certified by hand and seal. The choice mixed candies FIT FOR A KING fulfills the high demands of gourmets who like to spoil themselves."

Relishing a candy I was watching my neighbor in the window seat when the bearded man, who was dressed much too warmly, as I noticed at that moment, groaned and struck his forehead with the palm of his hand so loudly that for a second some passengers were startled and looked across at us anxiously. The heavy man groaned and called out rather loudly: "¡Caramba!"

"¡Caramba!" he repeated, and said one name: Borges. Then he pulled a passport out of his jacket pocket and proved to be an Argentine. He was born in Buenos Aires, I found out, but had avoided the country for particular reasons in recent years. He was an artist. He did not say musician, painter, or writer, he said only: artist. His gaze wandered here and there hungrily and got stuck on the legs of the stewardess, as he licked his lips sensuously. He talked about Buenos Aires and confirmed all the clichés that circulate regarding that city. His eyes began to undress the girl with shameless pleasure. Light turbulence shook the plane, as though it were stumbling along a meadow path. The plane turned to the left. The earth looked like a plate leaning to one side. There was talk about tangos and *avenidas*, the cheerful life-style, and passions, until I succeeded in interrupting that *suada* and asked about Borges.

"Oh, Borges!" laughed my neighbor. "Stop

bothering me about Borges. What do you know about Borges, anyway? What does mankind know about Borges? Borges is a mystery. If you even think of his name, you actually ought to cross yourself. Did you know that traffic stopped when Borges crossed the street? Then people said: 'There goes Borges!' What do *you* know about Borges?" And he laughed and fell silent and took a sip—from my cup!

"Stop bothering me about Borges! He was a man who lived his life only in books, nowhere else. He looked for knowledge and the secrets of the centuries, but only in books. And he did puzzle out one thing: that in the labyrinth of the power of the imagination there cannot be a final path. For Borges, reading was the only possibility of crossing the millennia. Just don't bother me about him," said the bearded, too warmly dressed, fat old man, and wiped the sweat off his face with a handkerchief from the breast pocket of his jacket.

"When Borges was writing," the Argentine informed me, "the burning curtain of his eyes shuddered. He wrote by heart. Because he couldn't sleep, he reflected at night, then he lived sentence by sentence, and when morning came, or only after weeks or months, he wrote down complete images and stories. Borges was crazy about metaphors, as Leopoldo Lugones had taught him, and he was therefore convinced that if what you wrote down expressed exactly what you wanted to say, then it lost value; you had to go beyond that. That's what happens with every old book: You read it beyond the intent it contains. And literature consists of not writing exactly what you plan, but in a mysterious or prophetic way going beyond it. Besides, what can be said indirectly has more power than what can be said directly. Anyone who notices similarities can construct his own metaphors. Of course, it would have to be someone who perceives relationships that aren't immediately conspicuous. And the metaphors would consist of expressing the secret connections between things. Because metaphor is equal to transference."

A young visitor to Borges once had written down after meeting him: "His eyebrows and eyelashes flickered in a lively way over his blind eyes while he was speaking to me, as though his eyelids, like sails under his brow, had turned into wings: The wings of his eyes that he sent forth like carrier pigeons, which he had circle around the whole world so that after their return everything could be reported to him over and over, so that nothing new nor old nor things to be discovered would escape from him into brightening concealment."

The fat stranger fell silent for a while, then he shrugged his shoulders, took another sip from my cup, and began to laugh in such a heartrending way that he jiggled and joggled.

"That's all well and good," I hear the old man say and see him slapping his leg; I hear him giggling, and he struggles for breath, "but there is no Borges. There never was a Borges."

It takes a while before the man calms down.

"The most promising candidate of all time for a Nobel Prize is a fiction. All that mysterious to-do about metaphors, metaphysical puzzles, and secret intricacies, black mirrors and labyrinths: pure nonsense, a pasted-up swindle from beginning to end, the mean parlor trick of a genial brain that takes the whole world for an idiot. What am I saying! Not a parlor trick, a masterpiece. There is no Borges, and there never was one. If you'll donate me your bottle of whiskey, I'll let you in on the secret. Listen! Not a glass. The whole bottle. You *do* have one. Don't deny it! I saw how you set yourself up with Black Label before our takeoff. So, how about it? Every one of us is corruptible in his own way."

I didn't hesitate a minute, fumbled in my carry-on, pulled out the nearly-full bottle, and set it down in front of the Argentine, who hastily opened it, filled his coffee cup a little recklessly, and gulped the alcohol greedily, then poured another right away. I noticed the fleshy and densely haired fingers of the old man, fingers that I had noticed previously only on painters of Madonnas. Again he wiped off his face with the little breast-pocket handkerchief. For a while he said nothing, looked out of the window dispiritedly, as though at a toy landscape, drank, poured again, fell silent again before he looked up at the ceiling and began to speak anew, loudly, as though he also wanted to convince our farther-seated neighbors of his words:

"Poetic memory, Señor, resembles a gigantic mirror in which actuality and imagination, truth, lie, and invention mingle. All the poets and works of world literature become shards of the name of a forgotten poet that is nothing more than a kernel in the mosaic of the aleph, that all-inclusive symbol to which the universe has shriveled."

The Argentine drank and was silent; he took a good swallow. "But, Señor," I interjected, "the biography of Borges, the figure whom I myself met…"

I got no farther, for the old man jammed his elbow into my side.

"Fraud, all a fraud, lies and deceit. There is no Borges. There never was one. The biography is made up, as the whole guy was made up. Don't make me laugh! A seven-year-old who already writes poems in two languages and at nine translates Oscar Wilde…. Believe that, if you want to! And there's more: His fleeting legendary childhood in a suburb of Buenos Aires, first on Tucumán Street, between Suipacha and Esmeralda, then on Palermo with its knives and guitars, the paternal library abundantly wound about with myth—all humbug, likewise his English grandmother with the grotesque name Frances Haslam from Staffordshire and her knowledge of literature, even his great-grandfather, said to have brought about the decisive turn in the War of Independence of 1824 in the Battle of Junín: 'Slowly, clad in a white poncho, he rode in the direction of the enemy lines, where two shots of a Remington brought him down. It stirs my power of imagination when I reflect that the firm that shaves me every morning has the same name as the one that killed my Grandfather.' Everything put on a little thick, don't you think?

"A man who claims to have inherited his blindness and his library from his father, and from his mother the touching gift of thinking the best of mankind, whom Jean-Paul supposedly bored and Schopenhauer fascinated, who claims to have read *Don Quixote* first in English, the *Divina Commedia* and Ariosto's *Orlando Furioso* in the streetcar on the way to work, and who owes to Macedonio Fernández, a tiny figure under a stiff black hat, the author of a novel with twenty chapters and fifty-six different forewords, the greatest of all gifts: learning to read skeptically.

"Ah, Macedonio: 'His genius survives only in a few of his pages; his influence was like that of Socrates.'

"None of it true, I tell you, everything from the realm of fable. Just stories, nothing but stories. Didn't this so-called Borges always maintain that reality first became accessible to him through the world of the book—naturally with himself as the glorious final goal of that long tradition, with himself as one who celebrated himself in poetry: 'At the end of fifty generations I return to the far shore of a great river not reached by the Viking dragons, back to the raw and laborious words that I, with a mouth turned to dust, uttered in the days of Northumbria and Mercia before I was Haslam or Borges.'

"Haslam or Borges.

"Ridiculous.

"Ridiculous, that pretended preference for Brahms and hourglasses.

"Ridiculous, that assertion of having bought in a rare-book store the eleventh edition of the *Encyclopaedia Britannica* with the first municipal literature prize.

"Ridiculous, the little anecdote about Christmas Eve, 1938: 'I ran up a floor and suddenly felt something scrape my head. I had run into a freshly painted open window frame. In spite of immediate treatment I got an infection and for a whole week lay sleepless every night, had hallucinations and high fever. One evening I lost my voice and had to be taken quickly to a hospital, where I was operated on at once. A sepsis had occurred, and for an entire month I hovered—without knowing it—between life and death. (Much later I wrote about that in my story *The South*.) When I began to recover, I worried about the intactness of my mind. Somewhat later I wondered whether I might ever again be able to write. I decided to write a story. The result was *Pierre Menard, Author of Quixote*.'

"By the way, that was the year World Champion Joe Louis knocked out Max Schmeling in the first round.

"Ridiculous, the legend about Sister Norah, presumably one of the most important painters in Argentina.

"Ridiculous, the universal history of dirty tricks: everything fiction, invention, fancies, out of thin air, lying to high heaven."

"So just: invented," I interjected, finally to get my peace, "but invented then by whom?"

The Argentine poured again with the trembling caution of a drunk.

"Listen, I was in the Calle Maipú, near the Plaza San Martín, the presumed residence of Borges. But I found no one at home. No wonder.

"As is well-known, Borges, with his friend Adolfo Bioy Casares, early on wrote crime novels and detective stories that were published under the resounding name BIORGES. Do you get it?! A combination of Bioy and Borges. The publisher was listed as: *Oportet & Haereses*, since *oporto* and *jerez*, port and sherry, were drunk preferably by Bioy. In addition there existed other pseudonyms such as Honorio Bustos Domecq or Francisco Bustos, where Bustos was an ancestor of JLB, Domecq one of ABC. And there were fabricated coauthors, all female, by the way: Delia Ingenieros, Margarita Guerrero, Maria Mercedes Levinson, B. Suárez Lynch. The B stands for Borges as well as for Bioy. Just between us, Borges created a believable female figure only once, in the story *Emma Zunz*. Otherwise he wisely and beneficially abstained from it. For that alone we must admire him.

"Concerning the secret of the collaboration it says in one note: 'I believe it promotes the common task of the ego, of ambition, and probably also of ordinary decency.'

"Critics called those books anti-Peronista crime satires. But who would ever trust a critic? The snobs and flibbertigibbets that appear in them are of no interest, rather three persons above all are:

"First, Don Isidro Parodi. That sounds, just between us, maliciously like parody. So Don Isidro Parodi sits in jail because of a knife fight. For his research the only things he has are his head and what his visitors bring him.

"Second, the great writer Carlos Anglada, author of the works *Hissing and Pissing* and—significantly—*I Am the Others*.

"Don't you notice anything yet?

"Third, Gervasio Montenegro, member of the

Academy of Literature, and, as such, naturally, a braggart, a Bohemian, heartbreaker, and actor—to be more exact, a second-rate comedian who lives from the income of a bordello that is operated by his wife, Princess Fiodorovna.

"Now note: detective, great writer, and actor. All one under the title: *I Am the Others*.

"That's saying a mouthful! As does the remarkable story that Borges repudiated his three early essays as youthful sins, had them turned to pulp, and forbade any sort of reprint. Everybody wonders, naturally, Why? Two short years before his official death, this supposed Borges confessed:

"'The world—unfortunately—is real; I—unfortunately—am Borges. Quite simply put, I would like to be someone else. Someone whom I don't know. I know myself too well. Life is a search for happiness. When someone looks for happiness, he finally comes to the realization that the only real persons are those whom he doesn't know. Reality is misfortune. Luckily, however, my memory is weak and I have gathered in only the happy moments. I have forgotten the sad moments. I have the expectation of dying soon.'"

The Argentine left me no lull.

"Just think for a moment what the name Borges means. It means bürger, borghese, bourgeois. That again is typical for Bioy Casares. Bürger Borges, a blind man, of whom Ernesto Sábato says that he could see better than any other person in Buenos Aires.

"But who even knows Bioy Casares?

"Or did you know, Señor, that he originally wanted to be a boxer or a world-champion tennis player, that he began to write very early on, and that his first work was a dictionary of synonyms?

"Remember: He loved synonyms, and so Borges is a synonym for Bioy Casares. At the age of four he imagined himself to be a horse and ate grass. He believed that through the cracks that sometimes open up in the earth's crust the devil could grab us by a foot and drag us into Hell. In addition, he was working on a perpetuum mobile, the Never–ending Rotation. His first volume of stories, *Caos*, reaps scathing reviews that advise Bioy to grow potatoes instead. He writes his notes in a pocket calendar, as I know, and he keeps talking about his little cinematographer.

"He divulged his narrative juggling acts in all the Borges stories, poems, and essays, and in doing so gave us the greatest gift that one can bestow upon someone one loves: telling a story.

"Games of hide-and-seek and riddles, the philosophical vaporous work, the search for the key, always unfolding like a detective story. It's always a matter of time and impermanence, of death and dream and doubles who are fictional figures of the protagonists, who in return are fictional figures of Bioy, the narrator, such as a Nils Runeberg, for whom Jesus is the double of Judas. And so on across all the literary genres, with the exception of the piece for the theater, because everything was theatrical for the actor Borges. And Bioy always narrated as though he himself were only a listener. The supposed Borges just repeats many of his stories, acting at the same time as though he had them secondhand—because the firsthand is Bioy.

"When I once had the rare opportunity to ask him personally about all these things, he gave me very revealing answers:

"'Time has taught me a few tricks: to prefer ordinary words to astonishing ones; to insert incidental details into reports demanded by readers these days, when reality is exact and the memory isn't; to tell the facts as though I didn't quite understand them.'

"We all do our best to be the heroes of trivial anecdotes.

"'I believe the fantastic means nothing more than to offer the reader a further possibility for the explanation of reality,' he said. 'I always liked inventions. So there are also spurious inventions in my literature. I live constantly with eight to ten ideas for stories and eight to ten ideas for novels. That is my wealth and my discomfiture.'

"Finally I took the leap and asked about Borges. Bioy smiled his reptilian smile while putting the following on record:

"'I met him in the house of my sister-in-law,

Victoria Ocampo. Borges already looked bad back then, and I still remember how he bumped a lamp and knocked it down. That was the start of a long friendship. Years later when a relative of mine, who owned a milk products plant, asked me to write something for him about yogurt, I suggested to Borges, who was in a bad way economically, that we do it together. And so, in my house in the country, we wrote a brochure about the advantages of yogurt. Because we were somewhat bored doing that, we thought about what else we might be able to write together, a sonnet, for example, with nothing but words containing *L*. Borges remembered a tale about a Dr. Prätorius who was about to murder children, by hedonistic means: he had them play and sing and let their exhaustion kill them. We practiced with things that we really did not want to write at all.'

"And then came remarkably frank words from Bioy, when he said:

"'Borges always treated me as an equal. There was no such thing as narcissism or vanity between us. I always had the impression that he was the incarnation of literature, a human book!'

"When I smiled skeptically, Bioy said to me with a true look of doglike devotion, 'I always try to be honest, even when I write fantastic literature.'

"My dear sir, no reader who has reflected on a tenth of what Bioy has thought about fiction is afterward the same reader of fiction that he was before. He will not only be a better reader, he will, above all, better understand the conventions of any literature.

"Bioy Casares, as the Pole, Lem, never tired of emphasizing, is a cynical heretic of culture by never sinning against its syntax—though, unfortunately, by no means as well known as Borges. At the same time he is extraordinarily clever. His love for ideas is beyond measure. Perfection is not linked to any format, but Bioy Casares achieved it by reconciling the unusual with the expected. Fantasy is no more than a bridge between one object and others. Just think of his novels *Fleeing* and *Sleep in the Sun*. Have you read his *Love Stories*? Do you know the *Book of Heaven and Hell*, that he supposedly put together with Borges? Do you by any chance remember the foreword, signed J.L.B. and A.B.C., Buenos Aires, December 27, 1959? *This book is a reincarnation of another, longer one. Every single one of the various holy books that mankind has conceived bequeathed us a very respectable number of pages*, it says."

Again the bearded man poured and wiped his face with his pocket handkerchief. The motors of the Fokker droned serenely.

"Has anything occurred to you? Didn't you really notice anything? Not even the initials A.B.C.? Who, two days after Christmas, on the Day of John the Baptist, writes a foreword to a book about Heaven and

Hell? That isn't significant? That should have no meaning? For a man like Bioy Casares? Do you even know that Borges never wrote a novel? And why? Because it is weary and tiresome nonsense to write thick books and for over five hundred pages extend a thought whose complete oral exposition takes a few minutes? Because Borges said that the novel was a form that would be surpassed, but not the story because it was so much older?

"No, because Borges never wrote a single line. Because there is no Borges.

"Every line that appeared under the name of Borges comes from the pen of Adolfo Bioy Casares. Born, by the way, in 1914. Like me. He published under so many pseudonyms that the extent of his work can hardly be established. He is in love with ideas; he sought, and what he found was the reality of Borges. Haven't I mentioned some of his wonderful books? Of course—one title you will have rightfully missed:

"*Morel's Invention*.

"Yes, indeed. That is the key to the mystery!

"Read that novel, Señor, and it will be as though scales fall from your eyes: Jorge Luis Borges is an invention of Adolfo Bioy Casares.

"Even Octavio Paz confesses: Borges was always the other Borges. And in that supposed Borges you can find the following note: 'Friendship is a conciliatory passion of the Argentine. One of the most important events ever in my life was the beginning of my friendship with Adolfo Bioy Casares. We met in 1930 or 1931, when he was about seventeen years old and I had just passed thirty. In such instances it is the rule that the elder is the teacher, the younger the pupil. That may have been so at the beginning, but when we began to work together a few years later, in actuality and secretly Bioy was the teacher. He and I embarked on many literary adventures.'

"Listen: many literary adventures, Bioy Casares the teacher—that confession alone ought to be sufficient to open your eyes.

"Ten years later Borges is supposedly Bioy Casares' best man.

"But Bioy achieved the realization of the greatest longing of all writers: not only to invent their figures, but to bring them to life. Not on canvas. No, to life. The sole objection: a writer, name of Kipling, may be able to think up a plot, but not to penetrate its moral. A biography can be invented. That's child's play— even the cynical praise of the caudillos Franco and Pinochet, even the bold assertion that democracy is nothing more than a curious misuse of statistics. All of that was put into Borges' mouth, and the approving columns of the Sunday illustrated eagerly picked it up. Everybody believed such nonsense. Some became indignant, others smiled sagely—perhaps because they were skeptical. Who knows? What did this supposed Borges, honorary Ph.D. of Oxford, Cambridge, Harvard, Palermo, and Crete, bring into the world? Nothing but fibs and word skirmishes, beginning with the assertion that in his house one would find not one book by him or about him, about the story of Great-grandfather Haslam, who wrote all his examinations at the University of Heidelberg in Latin and, during five years of study there, learned not one word of German; even the tale that he, Borges, had for a time been an inspector for the sale of fowl and eggs at markets. When he was young he wanted to be Hamlet, Raskolnikov, and Byron. Supposedly, together with Bioy Casares, he had even worked on a *Macbeth* translation. Maybe he also wanted to translate the *Communist Manifesto* into hexameters. Greek was his Latin, and he liked to read encyclopedias best of all. That braggart. And why did that gentleman never bring forth a novel? Supposedly because he couldn't give lectures but preferred dialogue. Typical regional theater. He was satisfied with writing forewords to books by authors who were unknown up to then. Only, his forewords had then made them famous, forewords out of courtesy, out of liking, but seldom out of affection. That comedian knew precisely, *In a good novel the characters are real, not the author.*

"With that, and with his blind attachment to detective stories, to Poe, and the mystic Swedenborg, he traveled around the world, and all the universities and intellectuals were taken in by him.

"But wherever he was, I bet he dreamed of Buenos Aires, a city whose inner courtyards are as concave as jugs. And he liked to flirt with his shyness.

"He, whose father, Jorge Guillermo, supposedly, in addition to being a lawyer and novelist, was a lecturer in psychology, and whose great-aunt—listen to this and marvel—is supposed to have been the founder of the *Instituto de Lenguas Vivas*. What a liar!

"Once he asserted in a conversation that I myself heard:

"'I believe that I am a very simple man. I say what I think. But since I thus contradict many prejudices, it is assumed that one of my jokes is involved. And so, well, my fame remains untouched.'

"I remember the words of that fraud precisely. And his memory was nothing but the memory of quotations, of pages, of what he had read. Supposedly he never got away from books. And as far as his personal story is concerned, that smart and life-sated Bioy Casares simply transformed the books he read into some plots and points. As soon as anyone asked Borges something about his life, he erred. He remembered only what he had read, but not what had happened to him. But maybe, in the final analysis, what happens to you has happened to someone else. Anyway, with time he lost his memory more and more. He was always very undependable when it came to dates, but the intellectual world thought that was amazingly interesting. The skies are darkened with dissertations, with Borges workshops in Oklahoma, with Borges as the witness of his academic sanctification. And with the academic hubbub and drivel, imitators and epigones came along. Possibly with good reason he tried to forget his past, he tried to live by projecting himself into the future. Or else he would have managed only a miserable existence, one like the lives of ordinary mortals. But the way it was, he could think only of victory when Waterloo came up.

"He never joked.

"His entire mendacious existence was a joke that only he could laugh at because everyone else was taken in by it. Again and again the gazettes spread his flashes of wit. For example: 'Poetry is born only of poetry.' Or: 'A tradition is not necessarily the imitation of something—above all it must be continuation and despair.' Nothing but platitudes, served up somewhat interestingly.

"Of course, he did eventually succeed in living his life the way Bioy Casares had sketched it out.

"Fiction is made by us, whereas reality is much rarer because it is made by someone else. That someone else is God.

"In our case, that God was named Adolfo Bioy

Casares. Consequently, reality must be much rarer. Seen in that light Borges was a man of action, that is to say, one who prefers the memory of his great deed and, best of all, lingers with that memory.

"I once mingled with journalists and critics who were permitted to ask him questions, and I asked Borges: 'What are your tidings?'

"'I don't have any kind of tidings.'

"Silence.

"'Tidings belong only to angels.'

"Everything that this devil brought into the world came from a book and ended up in a book. All the while, he wanted only to amuse, but never to persuade. It's enough to drive you crazy. And we—do you know, Señor, what we are?"

The Argentine now breathed heavily.

I shrugged my shoulders.

"We are the wasteland."

In that moment occurred the unexpected that belongs to every incident that comes to pass.

It happened with gruesomely precise suddenness and without any warning.

The motors of the plane stopped.

Both at the same time. All at once.

The plane was gliding.

It was gliding in icy stillness.

How to put my strangling into words, when very slowly and relentlessly the nose of the plane falls and the pilot, with his cigarette between his teeth, tries to pull back the stick.

He succeeds two, three times; then for long moments the machine lies again horizontal.

And yet quickly thereafter the next dive downward, and again the pilot pulls back, and again the Fokker lies more or less horizontal, but is already somewhat groggy, doesn't want to stay like that, dips forward, this time steeply.

Steeper than ever before.

How to describe the longing for a level, flat, swampy, springy rice paddy between Surabaya and Bandung, just a little swampy, to soften the impact, and not against a mountain slope, if possible, please.

How to describe that?

Just don't lower the landing gear. It would dig like a pitchfork into the field.

Brace yourself fast in your seat and grasp the seat arms.

Lean forward.

Your head between your legs.

Head down.

On your knees.

Tighten the seat belt.

Tight.

Tighter.

Until your abdomen hurts.

The loudspeaker:

Ladies and gentlemen, may we have your complete attention. We find ourselves in a situation that calls for discipline and complete cooperation.

No smoking.

No open flame.

But the captain smokes and puffs like crazy, pulls the plane back up again and again, tries to start the motors, but the propellers won't spin; no, nothing moves them.

Loosen your collar and tie.

Who's wearing a tie here? Not even my neighbor is wearing a tie, the pilot loosened his tie at takeoff.

Remove all sharp and pointed objects like ballpoint pens, glasses, dental prostheses, contact lenses.

Take off your shoes.

Hand luggage under the seat ahead.

Please remain calm and follow exactly the instructions of the crew.

Push forward the back of the seat in front of you, bend down quickly, and hug your knees tightly.

Hug your knees tightly with your arms.

Protect your face with the seat cushion.

Straighten up again only when the plane has come to a stop.

Only then loosen your seat belt.

At our signal leave the plane as quickly as possible and run away.

Run away from it.

Run away.
Please remain calm.
The nose tilts.
Comes up again.
Both propellers motionless and dead in the air.
The question asked again and again: What goes through your head at such moments?
Hug your knees tightly.
Mortal terror or summing up your life?
What kind of words are those?
What do they mean?
No, not a film before your inner eye, just:
Hug your knees.
Remain calm.
Run away.
More likely remorse, yes, remorse.
Or maybe not.
Perhaps deliverance, relief.
That everything will soon be over. Soon, soon.
Or the thought of that Japanese in a plunging jumbo jet, who was writing to his wife.
That plunging flight lasted more than twenty minutes.
That is a hundredfold eternity.
Cushion, face, seatback to the front, nose ahead, nose down, steeply, very steeply now, steeper and steeper, *run away from it.*
We have to count on several impacts.

With ballpoint pens, dental prostheses, ties, glasses.

The plane pancakes.

Hug your knees.

A strange fancy had taken possession of Almayer's brain.... It seemed to him that for many years he had been falling into a deep precipice. Follow the instructions of the crew exactly, *day after day, month after month, year after year, he had been falling; it was a smooth, round, black thing,* not a rice field, only mountains, gorge, yes, gorge, *and the black walls had been rushing upward with wearisome rapidity,* that's it, it's not us plunging, rather the world is hurtling past the plane windows: up, *a great rush, the noise of which he fancied he could hear yet; and now, with an awful shock,*

CRASH—

No: not a crash, a pop, a pop, and the right rotor catches, it starts, it's turning again, it's turning faster and faster, it's already turning so fast that I can no longer see how fast it's turning, finally I can't see it anymore, the plane catches itself, tips a bit to the side, but it catches itself at once, and another pop, two, three more false starts, and the left propeller also gets to work, tediously at first, slowly, very slowly, but then faster and faster and faster, come on, do it, dear God, make the propeller turn, yes, it's been turning now for a while, the plane is getting more stable, our captain is wearing the shoes of a waitress from a train-station café, with open heels, tied above the ankles, and he's smoking like a chimney, and Almayer, *he had reached the bottom, and behold! he was alive and whole.*

Almayer was uninjured, and the Argentine sat unmoved and wiped the sweat off his face with his dirty breast-pocket handkerchief. He clung to the whiskey bottle, holding it like a prayer book.

Unmoved.

For a long time it was quiet in the plane.

Glasses were put on, ballpoint pens pocketed, dental prostheses put into dry mouths, feet shoved into sweat-soaked shoes.

My Argentine looks at me and says: "A long time ago I decided to keep my involvement open."

"And Almayer," I yell, I yelled.

On the upturned face there was that serene look that follows the sudden relief from anguish and pain, and it testified silently before the cloudless heaven that the man…had been permitted to forget….

"Are you dreaming?" asked the old man.

Today is Thursday, and I'm dreaming.

By speaking inwardly to myself, I admit that I am dreaming.

Thursday, I dream.

It is a short, stubbornly repeating, fatiguing dream.

In the dream a simple man, son of an Englishman and a woman from Puerto Rico, is writing a few lines on a sheet of paper in the milky light of a winter afternoon in a little town named Rutherford, New Jersey, 9 Ridge Road.

The dream is exactly ten lines long, whereby the first line is written surprisingly only at the end. It consists of one word: Thursday.

The man writes the word finally, and with that the first line of my dream is also dreamed.

In the second line, which ends with a comma, just as the fourth and the seventh lines end with a comma (when I was going to school it was still called commata), in contrast to the sixth line, which ends with an open dash, while lines three, five, and nine stop with the words *like that, supported,* and *out*—so: the second line of my dream states: *I have dreamed my dream, as others have, too.* Where now I also put a period after *too*, because it's the rule, there is in my dream, as I said, a comma (or commata). I note that only because it's important to me not to let any sort of confusion arise and to relate my dream as faithfully dreamy as possible. Finally, the third line asserts the unheard-of. It says: my dream had *become nothing.*

At this point I am amazed in my dream that, despite the enormity I dream, I dare at all to continue dreaming. But in this and the following line it can be clearly read:

and so I stand here now, my feet planted in the soil, and look up into the sky.

The way the son of an Englishman and a woman from Puerto Rico in Rutherford, New Jersey, Ridge Road number nine, at this point in my dream can simply write *without care* will always remain a riddle to me, despite the milky light and the winter afternoon. At any rate after the word *sky* the writer in my dream puts a dash, presumably because he believes he owes it to a significant word like *sky*. Possibly he also thinks, however, of the next letters and syllables, which produce the following words:

I feel my clothes on me, the weight of my body in my shoes, the brim of my hat, the air that goes in and out of my nose, and I say to myself:

and at this very point I dream a colon, for it justifies totally what follows. Following it, you see, is something that requires a thoughtful pause introduced by a colon.

A deep breath.

Very calmly.

Now there follow, you see, those famous three words that constitute my dream, that, if I may say, constitute all the dreams of all people, and that state:

dream is over.

Period and no discussion.

For the sake of completeness I would like to note that recently I am prone to dreaming this dream ever more frequently. Even on days that are not Thursday. But then I am now no longer the seventy-eight-year-old son of an Englishman and a Puerto Rican in a small town named Rutherford, New Jersey, Ridge Road number nine, rather I am exactly as old as one happens to be from Thursday to Thursday.

Peacefully and evenly the Fokker lay in the air, as though nothing had happened.

Reconciled and resonant the motors roared.

Next to me sits the Argentine, who has found his way back to his favorite subject.

He is on Borges again.

"Where did we stop, Señor? Oh yes, we were interrupted just as I was about to speak about *Morel's Invention*. You want to know what follows from all of that? Very simple: The members of the Swedish Academy must have sensed something was awry. So again and again they hesitated with the Nobel Prize.

"What a triumph it would have been, had the poet Borges, invented by Bioy Casares, received the Nobel Prize for Literature from the hand of the king of Sweden. It would have been accepted by a second-rate comedian named Aquiles Scatamacchia, whom years ago Bioy Casares had once engaged from a regional stage for a single role that was to become the role of his life. All actors dream of receiving such an offer sometime. The actor had nothing more to do than portray a poet by the name of Borges, to recite the texts written by Bioy Casares, and to mime a poet who can sum up God and the world in a quote. Any pretty good comedian can do it: a bit of Shakespeare, a bit of Schopenhauer, the greatest from here and the choicest from there, no matter whether Swedenborg or the Merseburg magic formulas, like a museum director, a preserver of neglected trifles with which the attics of literary history are stuffed full.

"Borges once said, 'Reading is thinking with the mind of a stranger.'

"Only an actor can come up with such a sentence. The backwoods actor mentioned memorized world literature under the direction of Bioy Casares.

"But soon, because of all the reading, his eye problems began, and Bioy Casares at first could not figure out what to do with them. But then this ingenious man was able to make capital with it: the myth of the blind seer was born. His blindness did not reduce the Borges Project, rather it raised it into something like a cult. What a divine irony that bestowed both night and books! Cleverly circulated stories were the foundation, such as the one about his blind great-grandfather Edward Young Haslam—presumably his eye operation is documented in the London medical journal *Lancet*—or about his blind predecessors, directors of the National Library. And so Señor Borges commented on his blindness himself: 'Blindness is a seclusion but also a liberation, a solitude favorable for inventions, a key and an algebra. A significant consequence of my blindness was my renunciation of free verse in favor of classical meters. Obviously it is easier to recall verses than prose, and easier to recall regular verse forms than free verse. You can take along regular verse forms, so to speak. You can walk along a street or ride on a subway while drafting and ironing out a sonnet, for rhythm and meter have memorable virtues.'

"That's really a crazy comment on one's own blindness, when you compare it, say, with Sartre's jeremiads. Not a word of it can be true. It contradicts any kind of healthy human understanding.

"Jorge Francisco Isidoro Luis Borges, ostensibly born on August 24, 1899, in Buenos Aires, descended from Portuguese sailors and new Christians, editor of an anthology on brawlers and heroic knifemen, holder of several professorships, honored citizen of Buenos Aires, Gran Ufficiale, Commendatore, Commander of the Legion of Honor, Knight of the British Empire, fascinated by crimes and criminals, recipient of innumerable prizes and orders, among others, by the way, the Great Cross of Honor of the Republic of Germany, died on June 14, 1986, in Geneva.

"Don't make me laugh.

"In his last years the public had become accustomed to listening in on Borges. Every one of his steps was eagerly followed by the media. There is no list of everything that was written about him, and it would be fruitless to compile such a list. The austere face with a blind man's reptilian smile was known worldwide, his scandalous modesty had become just as proverbial as his relentlessness in revising and correcting his works.

"That was the last opportunity to make obscure as well as all-too-evident references to the questionability of his existence in forewords and marginalia, but the world wanted them on account of not taking notice any longer of his renown. Even in 1932 there was already the admission: 'Life and death have been absent from my life. From this impoverishment sprang a burdensome love for these trivialities.' By *trivialities*, of course, his *works* are meant.

"Or another example, when this bewilderment states, 'Our I is for us what is least important. What does it mean when we feel I? Where can the difference be between the way in which I feel myself as Borges and you yourself as A, B, or C? There is absolutely none. The I is what we share with one another.'

"Is that clear enough for you, the reference to ABC, to an I *that we share with one another*?

"*¿Comprende?*

"Presumably Borges died like his father: smiling and blind. But the actor simply left the stage. The texts from the pen of Borges are immortal.

"As stated: The key to the secret lies in the novel *Morel's Invention*.

"What a shame that no one wants to read that novel. I hope that the dreams in that book branch out further in the hospitable fantasy of all those who will close it one day.

"A.B.C. takes the game to an extreme, for he couldn't resist introducing his own novel with a foreword by Borges, whom he invented and who meanwhile achieved world fame, in which Borges praises Bioy Casares audaciously and closes his remarks, significantly, with the following words:

"'I have discussed the details of his fable with the author; I have read it again; it seems to me neither impertinent nor exaggerated when I describe it as perfect.'

"In the foreword to the novel, in which Bioy Casares shows his hand and demonstrates how he invented Borges, the invented Borges sets the novel of entanglement against the psychological novel, which is intended to obscure his character as a work of art woven with words.

"By the way, you find this argument again almost literally in the afterword that Borges wrote for the *Saga of the Beautiful Melusina* by Manuel Mujica Laínez: 'Future critics will find this novel of our imagination [again the all-too-evident reference to Biorges] irresponsible, a clumsy trick with rhetorical tensions instead of an offering of chronological events. That's sad, when it becomes clear that a careful study of the first, the opening sentences of *Don Quixote* could have spared us all this nonsense....' Overall, with this Pygmalion game Borges turns against the bellyaching that appears in our gazettes everywhere regularly at book fairs, that our century lacks the gift of tying interesting conflicts together and of conceiving an adventure in a novel, because it has become practically impossible to invent a new one. With the invention of Borges, Bioy Casares offers a brilliant counterproof and calls all the newspaper scribblers liars. With a lucky hand he ventured on an enterprise that may be counted among the most intrepid.

"How ineffectual, before such a background, is the criticism of Lem, the Pole, that Borges had felt the lack of a rich imagination from the beginning of his literary work; that is apparent from his adapting foreign material frequently.

"Lem understood nothing. There is no such thing as *foreign material*. The end of the story can be quickly told.

"The actor played the role of Borges and became world famous, which he would never have succeeded in doing otherwise. Bioy Casares remained modestly in the background, wrote the texts, and turned up the heat of his brilliant invention more and more. Until the attack. His income had meanwhile grown so that Bioy Casares was even able to buy a winery. Here is the proof."

And the Argentine circumspectly reached into his jacket pocket and pulled out a cork on which could be read: BORGES & IRMÃO.

"Now do you believe me?" asked the man with a laugh and showed his gold tooth.

"As he grew old Borges became wiser and wiser and thought about the many mountains that he hadn't moved. He even decided to write the presumably lost novel of his father, with the title *The Caudillo*, new and *undercover* as a merciless tirade against himself. But the novel remained a great longing if for no other reason than because of the military forebears on both sides of the family. The matter became really problematic only when Borges fell victim to the disease that all aging comedians fear: He couldn't remember the texts anymore. As a blind man he was forced to memorize the texts. Now his memory failed.

"What could he do?

"Bioy Casares thought of a remedy. A young and equally pretty and intelligent secretary was hired and was the only one let in on the secret: Maria Kodama, a Nippo-Argentine, who Ernst Jünger says in one of his eyewitness accounts became the alter ego of Borges and functioned in every respect as an organ attached to him."

"But in an Italian newspaper there was also something about an early marriage of Borges," I remembered from my stroll in Rome.

"Oh yes, right: Elsa Astete Millán. Immortalized in the poem *Praise of Shadow*, written at Cambridge in 1967. Elsa: the beloved of his youth, presumably rediscovered when he was sixty-eight. A trollop who negotiated honorariums with university presidents, $20,000 for a seminar, who delighted in displaying her mink, and who succeeded in getting a diplomatic post for her son from her first marriage until Leonore Acevedo de Borges, presumably Borges' mother and reader to him every evening—she died at ninety-seven(!)—put an end to her activities. She simply chased her off. Bioy Casares must have almost died laughing. The very first beloved, by the way, was named Beatriz (!) Viterbo: a Mardi Gras affair. Beatriz's brother introduced Borges to the mystery of the Aleph. And Maria Kodama when she was twenty…"

I remembered vividly the photograph of the widow in *La Repubblica* on the way to a Roman movie theater.

The whiskey bottle was almost empty.

The bearded stranger grabbed it in order to bring his story to an end.

"And a small miracle occurred.

"The grizzled Borges performer fell in love with Maria Kodama. When he saw his end approaching, he acted like a lonely millionaire. He married his secretary and bequeathed her not only the whole salary that Bioy Casares, in accordance with the contract, had paid him through all the long years, but also the rights to all the works by Jorge Luis Borges. Maria Kodama, however, swore on the Bible never and not under any circumstances to reveal the secret.

"But I know it.

"After all, I have read *Morel's Invention* again and again word for word and studied it closely."

The Argentine again wiped his face with his jacket handkerchief, looked at me with watery eyes, and after a time, with a strained voice and a thick tongue, remarked:

"Maybe Borges was ready to die, but who is, at whatever age? But the world will not hear one mortal word more from Bioy Casares about Borges. After all, he has already written the *Epilog* for the *Enciclopedia Sudamericana*, which is supposed to appear in Santiago de Chile in the year 2074.

"Perhaps he didn't want to wait that long, because two years after the death of Borges, Bioy published the highly revealing story "Caton" in *La Nacion* in Buenos Aires. Remarkably, it tells of an actor who performs the role of Cato, the Roman who resisted Julius Caesar when he crossed the Rubicon and was about to set up his dictatorship. Joseph Addison wrote a tragedy about that in 1713. But Bioy wrote about an Argentine actor who gradually becomes the flag-carrier of democrats who fight against tyranny. Time passes, the dictatorship collapses, he again plays Cato, and those who now applaud him are the same ones who during the dictatorship prohibited the freedom that they now applaud. Beyond any political reference that is a wonderful parable on the existence of Borges. Bioy left it at that. It's unnecessary to say anything more. For, as it says in *Morel's Invention*:

"'I have written a lot; it seems to me to be superfluous to quote parallels that come to mind, to mention doomed men who ready far-reaching plans for the future or in the moment of drowning see their lives roll past in all detail.

"'The last moment ought to be dismaying and confused. We are always so distant from it that we are unable to imagine the shadows that darken it.

"'Now I will stop writing and calmly consider how they probably turn off these motors. Now I am inclined to think of peace, of the joy of thought, of friendship and, even though this may sound all too ambitious, of loving and being loved.'"

A far green valley basin, surrounded by volcanoes, came into view.

Finally the roofs of Bandung.

The plane sat down gently, comfortably completed its roll, and finally came to a stop in front of a ridiculous airport building. The reverent silence in the cabin was broken by the clicks of opening seat belts.

There was a strong odor. Of sweat.

Incredulously I watched the man get up laboriously and, in embarrassment, with a smile, wipe his sweating hands on his jacket, turn to the open door, and promise me over his shoulder that there would come an age where there would be light, and mankind would waken from lofty dreams and find his dreams again—because he had lost nothing during his sleep.

On wobbly legs, we carefully walked down a small stair from the Fokker. The Argentine clutched his belongings. Sweat ran over his face.

"Read, Señor," he advised me urgently, "sometimes good readers are even more mysterious and rarer fellows than good authors. Anyway, reading is an activity that gives precedence to writing: It is more self-denying, more courteous, more intellectual. Keep reading your Conrad. After all, he found favor in the eyes of Borges. But don't forget one thing: Every text is an anthology put together by an author. All of world literature is a gigantic carpet of texts to which one can respond only by repeating them.

"Recurrence demands what belongs to it.

"And it is recognizable in that recurrence.

"It's not reading that's important, but rereading, renewed gleaning, re-creating, and creating anew.

"With unheard-of mania Borges researched a single theme: Man, lost in the labyrinth of time that consists of changes that are repetitions."

We were already on the runway, walking in the direction of the arrivals hall.

The Argentine went on talking steadfastly.

"Listen to what a smart fellow citizen confided to me—Andermatt was his name, or something like that:

"'The riddle will be solved only by being asked again.'

"That is the secret of the rare activity that seems to critics like a continual theft.

"Those simpletons have no idea of what else to do but to shout plagiarism or to drivel professorial prose.

"But, what isn't stolen hasn't been created.

"Only an imitation has a chance of ever becoming an original, in accordance with the respectable rule that knows only poison can cure poison, in accordance with the old saga hero who downs the eagle only with the arrow that was made from its own wing.

"Often a face hundreds of years old gazes at us for a few seconds from a new book. But often an old friendship does not hesitate to raise its visor all the way up and say its name.

"The origin of the subject matter of a novel is not as important as the use the author makes of it; everything depends upon the use he finds for it. The novelist, that voracious maw, needs everything in order to be able to go to work. (So-called plagiarisms are interesting only insofar as they represent references to a claim of totality, to a desire to serve all of reality as the subject matter without exception and scrupulously.)

"If Borges pointed out one thing, then it is this: 'Plagiarisms are interesting only insofar as they confirm genius.'

"Dreams? So what—if we are those who wake up the richer for them.

"Such universality disdains casting anchor.

"Without a mirror, no world.

"But, alas: These days, Señor, being well-read is considered an elitist outrage."

We waited for our luggage.

And even at the conveyor belt the old man called out to me over his shoulder that no mystery was worth as much as the ways that led to it.

I searched for my suitcase, and when I looked up again, the Argentine had disappeared. And there was nothing to be seen of the other passengers of the flight either.

I was alone.

And it seemed to me I was like the man who jumps on his horse and rides off in all four directions.

2

Potato Peelings

Since I could not sleep in the *Hotel Panghegar* on Jalan Merdeka, I tried to tell the story in a letter to Dr. Josef Stizl von Scharten, a manic depressive local historian in Thulsern with whom I corresponded now and then. Whether he received my mail unread is admittedly questionable, given the talents of the Thulsern mailman. He has the eyes of an owl, you see, and reads everything that passes through his fingers.

From Bandung I traveled on to Djakarta, from where a plane was to take me to Macao, my destination.

After my experiences with GARUDA, I decided to take the train. The stretch of rail between Bandung and Djakarta is among the most beautiful in the world. Any travel guide will confirm that. You travel like the king of England.

I was the only passenger in first class.

Slowly, like a giant of the ocean, the train moved along wobbly rails, snaked through the countryside, traveled across groaning and swaying bridges without parapets—images from films rose before my eyes and repressed what I was really seeing. When I wasn't looking out of the window, I became engrossed in my papers, settled down comfortably, took off my shoes, put my legs on the seat opposite me, and enjoyed having no one around me. Several times the friendly conductor asked me whether I wanted refreshments. I felt pampered and well on my way to getting over the shock of the flight.

I hauled the manuscript of my talk out of my bag to go through it once more. I had been invited to give a lecture on *Don Quixote* because I had publicly represented the theory that the novel was not by Cervantes, but rather possibly had been written by Shakespeare.

I have been taken by this idea since on a turbulent flight over the Andes I had found the following statement in Vladimir Nabokov's lectures: *Don Quixote is merely the shield bearer of King Lear.*

At that time the first notes came into being for the theory that, after I had presented it publicly to the scholarly community, eventually exposed me to derision, in the end scorn, and finally to total isolation.

They didn't want to believe me, they made light of me, and afterward wherever I went put me through the gauntlet. The whole conceited philological world slapped its thighs in amusement. My theory even found a place in the wastebaskets of the world press under *Curiosities and Miscellaneous*.

I made myself ridiculous. I made a complete fool of myself. Some call it idle fancy, others call it a malicious prank. But no one wants to believe me. Colleagues no longer speak to me. They avoid me. The worst, though, is their relentless pity. Their cynical, merciless pity. They even wanted to withdraw my right to lecture.

But my opponents cannot dodge the fact that Cervantes, like Shakespeare, died on St. George's Day in the year 1616. Even more: Shakespeare was born on the day he died, and he died on his birthday. Lacking imagination as they do, they merely neglected drawing the corresponding conclusions from that. Besides, that fact must have perplexed them as much as the fact that the great Shakespeare never published a novel. But for my colleagues there is nothing more obnoxious than imagination.

The modern age begins at the moment when Don Quixote de la Mancha leaves his village, goes out into the world, and discovers that the world does not resemble the one he has read about.

I was caught up in my manuscript:

He is called Alonso Quijano before he loses himself in the world of books. Not until *Don Quixote* is the whole world reading matter. From reading he is born and, in spite of his failure, he always returns to the book. Protected by a book he will still take windmills for giants without thereby losing the logic of his reading.

Don Quixote longs for reality without contradictions.

In that way he is the one who symbolizes the separation of word and object, whose accord he desperately seeks.

The fact that reality is not in keeping with what he reads allows Don Quixote again and again to transfer to reality the way he sees in his reading.

However, as soon as he accepted traditional reality, Don Quixote was condemned to die.

But that's why he lives on in his book.

Reading is the beginning and the end of Don Quixote's travels.

I quote from my lecture:

When he set out for the first time to challenge books to step down into life, he forced all of literature to follow him.

Don Quixote sees reason with the eyes of folly.

Nothing is dubious to him, rather everything is feasible. By reading he imitated the heroes in what he read.

When he is read, the world imitates him.

Don Quixote is a fool not only because he believed everything he read but because he believed that righteousness is possible, for his idea of righteousness is the idea of love.

He knows precisely that Dulcinea von Toboso is nothing more than a peasant girl. Nevertheless he loves her. And because he loves her, she becomes incomparable for him.

Because of that, Don Quixote loses his mind in two ways.

First through reading, and second when he is read.

On the one hand Don Quixote is the actor of his own adventures. Between the deeds of his adventures and the words there is no breach. For him, words and reality always agree because his reality consists of nothing more than words he has read.

On the other hand, Don Quixote discovers that he is nothing more than the theme of an apocryphal novel.

That is to say, for the first time in history a literary figure knows that he experiences his adventure at the same time it is written.

Don Quixote fails as a reader of novels because he wants to lead books into reality.

But as soon as he is himself the object of reading, he begins to conquer reality by infecting it with his reading.

But from this it follows, ladies and gentlemen:

Cervantes lets us open up the pages of a book in which the reader knows he is being read.

At the same time the author knows that he is being written.

Here begins the circle:

Borges is the author of *Pierre Menard* (Nîmes, 1939, dedicated to Silvina Ocampo, later the wife of Bioy Casares).

In Borges, Pierre Menard is the author of *Quixote*.

His work consists of the Ninth and the Thirty-eighth Chapters in the First Part of *Don Quixote* as well as of a fragment of Chapter Twenty-two. And Borges notes that the text by Menard and the text by Cervantes are identical, word for word; but the second is almost inexhaustibly richer.

Don Quixote is, according to Unamuno, the author of Cervantes.

Don Quixote is to Cervantes what the dreamer is to what is dreamed.

And who is this Cervantes?

He died on the same day as William Shakespeare.

Shakespeare and Cervantes were possibly one person.

I imagine it this way:

Cervantes' debts and struggles and sojourns in

prison, his whole biography, reconstructed by the fussy industry of scholars, were inventions, stories, lies that allowed him to disguise himself as William Shakespeare and write his plays in England, while the dramatist Will Shakespeare, the man with a thousand faces—from whom, significantly, not one line from a novel has come down, whereas there are known dramas by Cervantes—wrote *Don Quixote* in Spain.

Borges reports that Shakespeare, before or after his death, found himself in the presence of God and spoke to him:

"'I, who have been so many men, wish to be only one, myself.' The voice of God spoke to him from a whirlwind: 'I, too, do not exist; I have dreamed the world, as you, my Shakespeare, have dreamed your works, and in the images of my dream you are the one who, like me, is many and no one.'"

And if you do not believe me, ladies and gentlemen, I said to my colleagues, and if you consider all of this to be a fancy, then prove the opposite with the niggardly means of your niggardly profession!

But first read what Don Quixote himself said about this problem: *Believe in me! My heroic deeds are real. The windmills are giants. The herds of sheep are armies. And no woman in the world is more beautiful than the Empress of La Mancha, the incomparable Dulcinea of Toboso. Believe in me!*

You see, ladies and gentlemen, reality hasn't the

least responsibility to be interesting to you, just to us. Even a single repetition suffices to show what an illusion time is. Just imagine a card game in which you possibly repeat exactly the same tricks that were already taken centuries ago.

Except for our power of imagination we have no possibility of finding out what sorts of mysteries are hidden behind time. But we strive unerringly in our meager efforts to separate the lining from the gown in order to sniff around in it or like moths to lay our eggs.

And yet we can do nothing but always conduct our miserable research in the sweatbands of old hats!

The gap that we finally leave behind completely replaces us.

Whoever delves seriously into *Don Quixote* steps into the long shadow of Alonso Quijano.

Borges, too, recognized that when he said:

"All the literature of the past is a tradition; and in the best of cases we can perhaps attempt a few minor, extremely modest variations of what has already been written. We must tell the same story, but a bit differently by perhaps changing the tone, and that's all—but it's no reason for gloom."

They took particular offense at my notes on Thomas Mann.

You see, I was able to prove he erred in his *Ocean Voyage with "Don Quixote,"* a travelogue in which the exterior experiences of an Atlantic crossing by ship and the interior ones, grown out of readings on the trip, are so artfully woven together that they are mutually determined and heightened.

Here an error is involved that I commented upon, not in the manner of Wagner's Beckmesser, pevishly, pendantically, rather that I deemed typical of Mann. After all, Thomas Mann customarily liked to decorate his writings with often excessively rich documentation of his wide reading and his astonishing erudition, even in the remotest fields of knowledge, so that you often don't know whether you're reading a story or perhaps a learned essay.

To accept a strange judgment unexamined in passing—that temptation, which admittedly must be all the greater, the more unimportant the matter seems to be—overcame even Thomas Mann. He held forth on an author whom he quite obviously did not know at all or not sufficiently. My colleagues, and at the same time the so-called scholarly public, called me a crazy megalomaniac: to charge Thomas Mann, who read *Don Quixote* two times in a row, of such a thing could spring only from a sick mind. Here again the egg claimed to be smarter than the hen. In the final analysis philology was a serving discipline and Thomas Mann beyond suspicion.

I had no intention of putting Mann's thorough knowledge of *Don Quixote* into question. My objections concerned the spurious sequel—by the so-called Alonso Fernández de Avellaneda, concerning whom today hardly more is known than his name—about which Thomas Mann found hard words in his work and which, as I am firmly convinced, he could not have known at all from his own reading.

Thomas Mann spoke no Spanish. But now, as my colleagues immediately reproach me, Avellaneda's sequel had been translated into German. And, furthermore, actually twice.

I am so glad I possess both translations: *The New Adventures of the Knight Don Quixote, written by Avellaneda, translated from the French into the German language. Copenhagen 1707*, and *The Life and Deeds of the wise Knight Don Quixote de la Mancha. From the original manuscript of Cervantes, with the continuation by Avellaneda. In six volumes by F. I. Bertuch, Leipzig 1775, Volumes 5 and 6. New edition Carlsruhe 1785.* Unfortunately, I own only the second printing; only three copies of the first are known, all three in public libraries, and thus unobtainable. Since then Avellaneda has not again been translated into German.

Thomas Mann does praise the *Don Quixote* of Cervantes, but he writes about the "so-called Avellaneda": "This sequel, to which a speculative dabbler let himself be tempted by the worldwide success of the novel, saw Don Quixote as nothing more than a fool worthy of being lashed, Sancho only as a glutton."

Thomas Mann calls the pseudonymous author from Tarragona, in the language of our newspaper critics who specialize in snobbery, a dabbler, and his work botched.

An exceedingly harsh judgment.

I became suspicious that he had never read him.

It's a fact that both the German translations of the false sequel go back not to the Spanish original but to a French translation. It comes from Alain-René Lesage, the same man who wrote *Gil Blas*, and it's really more a free adaptation. From the genuine second part of *Don Quixote*, the one that Cervantes brought out one year later, Lesage took over into the false sequel not only the conclusion, in which the hero dies, but also that great idea of the reflection of the doubled Hidalgo, so that in Lesage's Avellaneda and also in the latter's German translations that very play of doubles occurs that entertained Thomas Mann so much in the genuine *Don Quixote*. Since Mann neither spoke nor read Spanish, he could have read Avellaneda only in Lesage's version or in one of the two German translations, and he would then have had to assume that Avellaneda and not first the famous Cervantes...

In any event, one must consider that Cervantes wasted little thought about who may have hidden behind the name Avellaneda. He pretended that solely the reference to his age and to his crippled hand had aggrieved him personally, though not literarily. Of course Avellaneda did not omit mentioning the fact that *Cervantes* in the Golden Age meant *the horned man* (the family coat of arms of Cervantes depicts two stags with splendid antlers)—also in the literary sense. Nothing new under the sun: In Italy Ariosto with his *Orlando Furioso* reacted to the challenge set by the *Orlando Innamorato* of Boiardo. *Lazarillo de Tormes* could refer to just as abundant offspring as *Celestina*, and Gaspar Gil Polo continued the work *Diana* by Montemayor with a *Diana Innamorata*. Even in 1602 a certain Mateo Luján de Sayavedra had published a *Second Part of Guzmán de Alfarache*, even before Alemán himself had finished his work. Alemán was so outraged that in his second part he introduced a character named Sayavedra, a vagabond and liar who first burglars Guzmán, then becomes his servant, finally goes crazy, and in the end drinks himself to death.

For almost four centuries the identity of Avellaneda has been sought without success: Mateo Alemán was suspected, as was Lope de Vega, the duke of Sessa Bartolomé de Argensola, the Dominican Juan Blanco de Pax, and Friar Luis de Aliaga, the confessor of the king.

Why Lope de Vega? Avellaneda, in his prologue, reveals himself as a follower of Lope, for whom

Cervantes was merely a *lego*, a lightweight. Cervantes did not like that enterprising showoff and ladies' man, who wrote verses in praise of himself and subsequently set down the names of his lovers under them.

On the basis of Cervantes' own references, Jerónimo de Pasamonte, that scribbling and rosary-doting soldier who served Cervantes, finally was believed to be recognized as the model for his Ginés.

Be that as it may, even in the preface of 1605 Cervantes says expressly that he was only the stepfather of his hero, and in the course of the story he always takes shelter, as even Canavaggio points out, behind various narrators. Finally he announces new adventures of his hero without, however, having announced anything about their narrators.

I think that Cervantes himself built a golden bridge for the unknown imitator. Even the preface to his own part is clear, when he turns to his reader and says: "You would like it very much for me to call him [Avellaneda] dull-witted, simple, and shameless; but nothing of the sort occurs to me.... By the way, consider that one writes not with his gray hair but with his reason."

Cervantes advised his reader, should he accidentally encounter this Avellaneda, to inform him that he does not consider himself insulted and knows very well "what the temptations of the Devil are, and that one of the greatest is to give a man the idea that he can write a book and have it published, and by doing so he can win as much fame as money." Thomas Mann calls that "Christian and nice," but he did not understand the ambiguity with which Cervantes here refers to himself. On the other hand, a hint of it in Thomas Mann cannot be denied—after all, he dreams at the end of his ocean trip, faced with the towered giant city of Manhattan, of Don Quixote appearing to him— admittedly under the name of Zarathustra: "He was so gentle and polite."

Now, every adventure in Avellaneda, however, ends with disappointment, and the two heroes, from whom Jumping Jack and Merry Andrew came into existence, press on to their dreary end.

Let us just consider it, ladies and gentlemen, a violent end would have been just as unbelievable for Don Quixote as a peaceful old age.

So what if Cervantes had thought up the alternative to his work himself and had consciously gone beneath his niveau? It brings any writer satisfaction when the most incisive squaring of accounts comes not from the pen of a critic or colleague but from his own. Only in this way are the invectives in the foreword of Avellaneda comprehensible.

So what would have happened, if...? That would have confused philology, but not Avellaneda, whose greatest purpose and benefit in the last analysis would have been not only to let the knight, Quixote, win back his identity but to spur Cervantes on to his highest accomplishment; he entrusts his own novelistic hero with the task of taking the apocryphal Quixote into the crossfire of the narrator and his heroes.

And it seems to me that Thomas Mann, with his equally hurried and harsh judgment, did not consider that.

For me it wasn't a matter of maintaining justice—I am no Kohlhaas—although it naturally pleased me to be able to tweak the nose of such a famous man. What pained me was Mann's opinion about Avellaneda. For even if he admittedly falls far behind the great Cervantes in worth, he is still not so bad that he has to be snubbed in the language of our literary critics. Confronted with genius, a man easily becomes a dabbler, who otherwise, all in all, easily holds his own. If he had really been so bad, would his deception have been believed in all of Spain? No, if the real hidalgo is magnificent and the genuine double sublime, then the false one is still worth reading and the false double is a dangerous knight.

If Thomas Mann were still alive, I would gladly send him Bertuch's translation, even though it is only the second printing. For the doubled false hidalgo is doubly doubled: I own him in two copies. Unfortunately, both only from the second printing.

Sometimes in my boldest dreams I imagine that I had met Thomas Mann and had not only presented him with my reflections but also had been allowed to make him this gift. But then my thoughts take flight. I see myself leave Kilchberg, but see Thomas Mann pouring himself a glass and toasting himself: He had after all managed to remain silent and allow me my triumph, which was no triumph. Concerning the value of Avellaneda we would admittedly have kept our different opinions. For in the library of the necromancer, so I dreamed on occasion, was a manuscript bound in blue-dyed leather, a rare item: the never-published handwritten translation of Avellaneda, done at Strasbourg in the year 1662 by Anonymous.

I laid my papers aside, stared for a long time out of the window, and thought about everything that the fat Argentine had told me. And since I always like to read several books at the same time, I exchanged Borges for Conrad.

His words seemed to confirm the explanations of my rare neighbor on the plane as well as the behavior of my colleagues, who had become my enemies:

You don't understand that. But then how could you? —with solid paving stones under your feet, surrounded by nice neighbors who are ready to applaud you or attack you, wandering thoughtfully between the butcher and the police, in holy terror of scandal, the gallows, and the insane asylum—how could you imagine into what special primeval regions unhampered feet could carry a man simply because of his solitude—of restless solitude, supervised by no bailiff—as the result of silence—restless silence in which the warning voice of your neighbor, whispering public opinion, could not be heard.

And while I was lost in these sentences, suddenly the train gave a jerk and slowly came to a halt.

It stopped on level ground, and at first I heard nothing, then yells and screams. They sounded very excited, they sounded full of terror. But I sat comfortably in my compartment, my legs stretched out, a refreshment on the little table. I didn't give the incident another thought.

A little while passed before my compartment door was thrown open and two conductors threw a bundle on the floor at my feet.

A long-drawn-out whistle of melancholy drove the locomotive on.

I looked up from my reading and recognized in the sweetish-smelling bundle a horribly mangled man, who had been struck or run over by the train. His skull was sticky with blood, and at one part it seemed open; the slim man's upper-left arm was sliced open; his chest was crushed, and his backbone was twisted grotesquely, as though a great force had tried to turn it into a spiral.

I characterize this incident in my life as the unheard-of event that came to pass.

From now on I could look out for myself.

Suddenly one is dragged through the dust on his back, the back of his head bumps along, and ultimately he is hanged up by his guts.

I recognized myself and my life in the sight of the bundle in my compartment, and the scales that had plagued me until that moment fell from my eyes.

Still, and for that very reason, I continued my trip.

In Singapore, Changi Airport, I had a half-day wait and decided to follow a poster that offered a tour of the city for passengers en route. Hardly had I appeared at the window when I had to surrender my passport. After about fifteen minutes a wiry female sergeant appeared in the shape of a lady guide and handed every participant a small round sticker. I was at once instructed to put my sticker higher on my lapel so that it would be in plain view for various policemen. The way to the bus led past numerous checkpoints that were accompanied by fairly long waits. Finally we were seated in the bus and the city tour could begin. While the female sergeant was commenting on the road into the airport, which could be transformed into a runway by the rapid removal of the palms that all stood in barrels, the first instructions flowed out with her comments. Above all, spitting in the bus was prohibited ($50 fine), and we were cautioned to show our gratitude to the government that had allowed this particularly generous arrangement exclusively for guests in transit. Afterwards came about half an hour of explanations about what was prohibited in Singapore: crossing the street at an angle and not at the zebra-striped crossings, throwing away cigarette butts, throwing away paper trash. Each time the appropriate fine was mentioned: $100 for not flushing after using a public toilet. Mixed in with this index of punishments was information about the prosperity of the country, about apartments with showers and commodes, about the common rooms that brought together the youth of both sexes who belonged to particular social levels—at the time the state allowed one and a half children—about the modern harbor, and the elimination of poverty and slums. Punishments and accomplishments balanced one another out, and the female sergeant kept on talking unswervingly. In Chinatown the passengers on the bus were permitted to leave for ten minutes of sightseeing at a pagoda. Anyone who did not get back on, we were warned, would become a guest of the state police. But everybody came back. On the way back to the airport, which led past the old Raffles Hotel—at the time in the middle of a renovation—in which Joseph Conrad had stopped off, the total fines for misdemeanors in Singapore increased and finally ended, shortly before Changi Airport, with the frequently repeated reference to execution by hanging for the possession of drugs. The female sergeant concluded her two-hour tour with the words: "Ladies and gentlemen, I hope you have enjoyed it and that you will soon come again to Singapore."

It smells like a slaughterhouse.

Thousands of chickens and ducks are being slit open, disemboweled, and scalded.

Palm readers and fortune tellers have established themselves in the quieter corners.

In front of the official residence of His Excellency the Governor, the red and green flag of Portugal hangs limply on its pole.

Under the trees of the coastal promenade elderly Chinese in short pants and undershirts gather.

Out on the dirty-brown waters canoes and junks are zigzagging.

Blossom time is finally approaching its end.

The deadline is December 20, 1999.

Then Macao will belong to China again.

The inheritance is a city that has sold itself to chance. Macao's erstwhile masters ruled badly; they ruled like the bamboo that bends in the wind.

Macao has no future. Macao is a wart on the fat belly of China. The glory of days past is faded, peeling off, decaying, sinking into oblivion.

That is the place that he selected for the end. Catchall place for those in flight and for adventurers.

The last European bastion across the seas.

A place, a city, in its last throes once again roused by baccarat and blackjack, by greyhound races and roulette.

In reality having dwindled into sheer meaninglessness. Tired and exhausted.

His place.

Here he had finally understood it, here it had become comprehensible to him, vivid:

All is in vain, and one must at least have the courage to have no pretenses.

But it was this very courage that he did not have. He always had pretenses.

Macao was his last pretense.

Anyone who trusts his own eyes has himself to blame.

Macao's remoteness furthered my/its supernatural serenity, furthered the sleeping sickness, furthered the patience that perhaps was called resignation.

The professor said to himself: Anyone who has no neighbor is disposed to monologue. And in a monologue, according to old precepts, there are no lies.

There was an odor of dried cod and roasted coffee, and he looked into many a corner and damp building; he looked into hospitals from whose windows bones flew; there was an odor of vinegar in the alleyways, and they opened themselves up to him like cracks in the earth.

Arrogantly I recognized in myself, and he recognized in himself, a specialist in the conjuration of shades.

Macao was of help to him in this.

Again and again he saw the same film that this city flickered before his eyes:

The lost empire, the futility, the end.

Sure, he could book *saudade* in any travel bureau. Mania for the indelible hurt, the enjoyment of an unspeakable misfortune, the hope for despondency. He was acquainted with those.

Portugal was the only country in which grown men built their insignificance with a howl.

As he had once been informed when he took this as his area of specialization.

"All peoples have their kitsch and their accolades. But no one believes in such nonsense as much as we do. Kitsch is our religion. It is the halo for our ignorance, the gloriole that we set upon our misery. In the whole world only we are proud of being doomed."

A Portuguese ear, nose, and throat doctor had said those sentences to him.

And that is why he, that is why I, became a Lusitanist.

The *Lusitania* sank, struck by the torpedoes of the German submarine U-20, on May 7, 1915, and with it close to two thousand people, predominately women and children. Crown Prince Wilhelm expressed his "great joy" about it to his imperial father; the newspapers fell all over themselves in cynical triumph; the lies about the munitions on board the passenger steamer served as a justification.

Lusitanics is the science of loss.

And suddenly I recognized myself, he recognized himself, as an essential part of that chimeric world empire.

The voices in his head fell all over themselves. He grabbed his brow, held his skull with both hands, and wished for only one thing: to be freed of the swarm of hornets.

He looked up, and he saw clocks everywhere. Clocks on towers, on market halls, on store corners. They seemed to me as though they had originated in a time when clocks were something expensive, something rare. But then I discovered that all the clocks were wrong or had stopped. No one wound them up anymore; many had only one hand and offered him time travel, as he imagined it: time travel gratis.

The year on the calendar, what did it mean? The clocks let him tell through which time zones he wandered, what crevices and repudiations history showed.

Macao seemed to me like olden times.

He was not in the Now, rather I sensed a trace of ancien régime, a mixture of enticement and horror.

In the small shops he discovered boxes that had

been packed fifteen, twenty years before. The last Portuguese enclave was still waiting for that King Sebastião, who had been loved not for his successes but for his defeats. They waited for him until one day, supposedly on a foggy morning, he turned up, because against the will of his counselors he had decided to begin a hopeless, belated crusade in August 1578; in the middle of the desert, the nags still seasick from the crossing, he suffered that catastrophic defeat that swept along almost all of Portuguese nobility. The crown fell to the successful Spaniards, and the king himself sank into the godforsaken wadi, where he has been lost for more than four hundred years, waiting for a return.

And I imagined my life to come: an old-fashioned gentleman in a palace hotel that demanded humility, high over a lake, for such a lake has something corrupt about it, taciturn, inaccessible, far away from everything, but not unworldly, with ritualized habits, a collector of bizarre masks, hats, and walking sticks, fanned with the coldness of solitude, a gentleman who had scoffed away all pain from his world, an eccentric whose age had granted him the favor of returning to his lost, never-lived childhood so he could spin the yarn of history in solitude and say arrogantly: Speak, Memory. No one would miss him, if he were one day no longer there.

That's how I imagined my old age.

But the hole we leave behind finally replaces us completely.

With these words he had ended his lecture, expressed his thanks courteously for the attention of a mostly speechless auditorium, and had gone from the air-conditioned, half-darkened hall out into the heat. Alone he walked down the stone stairs, heard his steps, sweated profusely, although he had gone only a few yards.

And while he imagined that he would one day be washed up in this city whose edges were frayed, ragged, and decayed, and be devoured by the birds, I decided to write home.

In my thoughts I was already opening my writing kit, he was already smoothing out the letter paper, unscrewing the cap of the pen—I'm in love with that sound—he was already putting a date on the upper-right-hand corner, which one seemed of no importance to him. I was already beginning with the request with which as a child he had plagued his father again and again on detested Sunday strolls:

"Father, tell me what grass is. Father, tell me why it will always grow back. Father, explain grass to me, please."

But then he closed his eyes and surrendered to what he dictated to himself. My thoughts seemed to me as though they would drip in thick beads of sweat from his head along his neck into his collar, down his shoulders, chest, and back, downward until they would be lost in his shirt, absorbed by the material that, as soon as he had arrived at his hotel, he would have to toss into the trash can and immediately afterwards shower for a long time and thoroughly.

He said his name aloud, as though someone were about to interrogate him.

Family name, first name, place of birth, date and year of birth, occupation: Professor of Lusitanics, no, he had nothing on him except for his lecture on *Don Quixote*, which he had been invited to give, and a book, which book, a collection of reports of shipwrecked persons that was part of his work he intended to publish, a new edition, *Reports of Portuguese Survivors of Shipwrecks, recorded by eyewitnesses, edited by...*, here, look yourself, see for yourself.

He would surely be washed up, an unidentified corpse, gnawed to bits by fish and birds, with hollowed-out eyes and melted limbs, washed up, driven onto land by the play of tides, acquiescent and completely unimportant, for the dead eyes would no longer recognize the silhouette of Macao that gradually disappeared into a colorless morning fog.

But in reality it was midday, I was alive and sweating, going my way without a destination. No, he would not write the letter home. When he read the letter he had written to the end, he still felt miserable, because I had always imagined my lines to be more perfect.

Only since I drank the rat poison do I know really how big the world can be when you are looking for something you lost. And wherever you may go on your search, you are always already there. The traveler is a bird that travels with his cage. Even on the Rua da Praia Grande, the grandest street of Macao. As though totally deserted it lies there in the heat of midday; no breeze hangs in the emptying banyan trees; nothing moves, everything stands and waits. Old men hold fishing poles in dough-colored water, adolescents hang around apathetically, a few yards away a handful of children play cards.

Macao is a den of gamblers; even the smallest children are infected by the fever. Two or three streets farther on the Hotel Lisbon rises as a mighty, frozen-concrete cake. The rooms there are always taken. Hong Kong Chinese arrive in packs, gamble and sleep in shifts, crowd around the felt-topped tables of the hotel casino, shove the colorful chips back and forth, throw them like hopes onto the felt, settle and wait to see where the ball rolls, scribble illegible notes on mysterious betting sheets, look for quick and sure luck at baccarat, blackjack, and roulette, leave the hotel only to traipse around to pawnshops on the Avenida Almeida Ribeiro before they return in a short hour by jetfoil, a jet-driven hydrofoil over the Pearl River to Hong Kong, where they disappear as nameless ants into the anthill, back to a neon-lit workplace where imitations are manufactured. Most gamblers buy their return tickets when they set out on the trip, while they have the cash. But many, when even the return ticket is finally lost, must look around for a money-lender, to whom they guarantee more than a hundred percent interest.

I, on the other hand, bought my ticket at the *farmacêutico*. What do I care about the gamblers, or about the colorfully loaded clotheslines over the narrow lanes, or the countless handicraft booths that stink of camphor wood and cookhouse brew! What does the usual market tumult matter to me, or the shoving and crowding, or the specialties of Macao that are palmed off on the tourists: ants, chicken claws, monkey and snake meat! Supposedly, everything that has four legs ends up in the cooking pot here, unless it's a chair, and everything that floats, except a U-boat, and everything that flies, except a helicopter. That's what the tourist guides announce when they rave about the mysteries of Chinese cooking and pull the money out of the pockets of the naive.

What do I have to look for here, what have I lost here?

Wherever I travel, I am already there.

So on to the cemetery: walled in by the narcotic aroma of blooming frangipani trees, where the young dead lie: The Right Honourable Lord Spencer

Churchill, Dr. Robert Morrison, who translated the Bible into Chinese, and F. G. Schnittgers, born at Pleuhn in Holstein, died on May 31, 1773. It doesn't say of what. Maybe he, too, had a pharmacist advise him. There's one man, a certain Johann Friedrich Ipland from Apenrade, who lies under two gravestones: His widow sent a stone for him from Europe, because of her suspicion that the one in Macao might crumble too quickly. There are sufficient places in the oldest foreign post of Europe in East Asia to be comforted: the gardens with the grotto of the poet Camões, who lived here, the countless churches, for on the peninsula of Macao there are more churches than in Vatican City. The six-inch-long bone from the left arm of St. Francis Xavier can be seen here, and dog races rollick in the Canidrom on the Avenida General Castelo Branco. The history of Macao offers everything that can please a European heart: from the opium smuggling via the Jesuits, who with the help of Japanese artisans built the façade of St. Paul's Church, to the Taoist A-Ma Temple, where the future is predicted with smoke sticks. A-Ma-bau, Bay of the Goddess A-Ma. Macao was derived from that. Curry, pepper, and coriander determine the aroma; from the empty window recesses grins Portugal's past. In the seminary of San José lodges the grizzled monk Pater Manuel Taxeira, who has written a hundred books on the history of Portugal in Asia.

But all that has nothing more to do with me, not the lighthouse, not the fortress, not the Pousada de São Tiago, the most exclusive address on the peninsula.

I live in the Hotel Bela Vista on a hill over the ocean. The paint is peeling from the façade, the wooden floor has become dull from the eternal polishing, the boards creak, the fans on the ceiling have long since decided not to turn anymore. Anyone who takes breakfast on the sloping hanging balconies must expect them to collapse at any moment. *Hotel Bela Vista, 8 Rua do Comendador*, it says on the white-and-green paper matchbooks. And on the reverse:... *a century of experience.*

My residence.

The hotel seems abandoned. No one is at the reception desk, not a waiter can be found. I call out but I receive no answer. Finally I walk through the salon, from the walls of which the dismal gazes of Portuguese noblemen from the Bragança line follow me.

In the kitchen I find a fence-lattice-thin Chinese woman peeling potatoes. Her weary eyelids lift up only briefly, the old woman seems to peel potatoes as though she were asleep.

What she peels off is my story. The potato peelings are the rolls of film that begin on this day in Macao that is mowed down by heat.

As though in a trance the Chinese woman turns

the potato in a wizened hand. In the other she holds the knife. It doesn't move. The potato turns. The knife is brazen, rigid law, the potato the world that turns, no, that's turned by a shriveled hand so that its skin can be pulled off: Peeling by peeling, film roll by film roll. The motionless, indifferent face of the woman expresses that law. Does the old woman know that I had my palm read at the grotto of the poet Camões? Does the Chinese woman know what the fortune teller, who had the same shriveled hands as the potato peeler, confided in me, for a sum? Did the old woman listen in, or was it, in the end, her husband or her brother, who for his part knew that his sister, his wife, would peel off my film?

There was talk of four mountains: four mountains that I had to cross. Four, not seven, as is customary. The first mountain is called Illusion, says the fortune teller, and he looks at my open left hand tensely for the lines that he carefully traces with fingertips yellowed from smoking. The second mountain is the Mountain of Rebellion, because you will soon recognize that the illusions with which you arrived simply load you with a new mountain. You will rebel and want to take everything in hand yourself as a rebel: against everything and everyone. But rebellion, too, is an illusion, Sir, that loads you up with the third Mountain of Resignation. You will be disheartened, give it up, not want to keep fighting, will tumble downward, farther and farther, onto the peak of the fourth mountain. That is Death. But the fourth mountain and the first are confusingly alike. Until finally you will not know whether you have arrived on the Mountain of Death or again on the Peak of Illusion.

That's what the fortune teller had said and with a smile closed my hand, but opened his own for payment for such an oracle.

The Chinese indifferently peeling her potatoes glances up. In her eyes is mirrored the Square of Heavenly Peace. How many people die in that very place I cannot count, but I see them collapse, I hear the shots and the bursts of fire, I see the tanks rolling and the soldiers coming from the Forbidden City, and the closing, obstacles that surround the splendid four-lane thoroughfare. In the glare of the searchlights the slaughter wouldn't stop. In the midst of it bicyclist rickshaw drivers venture forth. Bodies smeared with blood hang from the potato peelings. The fiery glimmer of a burning army vehicle makes the eyes of the Chinese woman flicker and the paring knife flash. And again rifle fire begins, people flee head over heels, running for their lives, cringe with pain like dead men, here the enclosure of a hotel building, there a gaping head wound, blood running over a young face, but the Chinese woman peels her potatoes, is struck by a ricochet, a shot gone astray, but she doesn't simply sink down, but continues peeling, in spite of the snipers on the roofs and in the windows of houses opposite, peels in the name of the State Party and peels in the name of the defenseless students, peels in the emergency room of a hospital, where doctors in smeared surgical gowns and nurses with faces torn with grief climb over lying, squatting, and groveling people, foreign reports tell about potato peelings on the Square of Heavenly Peace, talk about the four hundred badly wounded and about more, those shaken by weeping won't be quieted, collapse unconscious, tumble to the motionless bodies that lie everywhere among the potato peelings, a child is there, too, with a half dozen bullet holes, a child, numerous children, women who sob and demand only one thing of the reporters: that they write about it, they have to write, they must tell everybody what they've seen here so that the whole world finds out, the whole world must learn about this orgy of potato peeling, they must tell about the People's Army of Liberation, for that's its real name, which slipped into the city like a thief and then just shot and slaughtered, and we sat there like the pieces of a board game and wanted to peel potatoes, but then the army took the knife in its hand and began to peel, the fast vehicles of the infantry, the tour buses with soldiers in bright shirts in civilian clothes, the Jeeps that simply ran over people and kept going, like tanks, too, laying their tracks over people, they had to tell about the battering and stabbing weapons used for peeling potatoes, about the strangling chains and tear-gas projectiles that struck some of us right in the face, they have to write about the clothing that's stained and about the corpses that cover the Square of Heavenly Peace and hang between the barricades while a new convoy rolls up, from which shooting is coming, from which there are those aiming at the backs of the fleeing people, and hitting them, really hitting them, a tank drives over a bicyclist, only the bicycle crackles, leaving him lying squashed in a puddle, at midnight the gates of the Great Hall of the People and the gates of the Zhongshan Park bordering the Emperor's Palace, we see from the Peking Hotel, like a dark streak, only the silhouette of those who block the boulevard to the east and fire their rifles into the mob of people. In the hours until dawn the noise of battle increases more and more, more and more potatoes are being peeled, behind a dozen heavy battle tanks trucks, spitting out wild salvos, roll to the square past the eyes of the Chinese woman peeling potatoes indifferently. Anyone still on the square falls, anyone who can still run runs for his life, which will come to an end in a side street, and the runner doesn't even know it, although he's had a hint of it for a long time. And later the personnel cars are parked properly in rows, and a squad tries to clean the Square of Heavenly Peace of the potato peelings lying everywhere. Tanks are still moving over the tent city of the students, in double rows the soldiers proceed against the occupants of the Heroes Memorial, and over the radio it is announced that entering the Square of Heavenly Peace is prohibited, television shows a battle tank ramming and knocking over the Goddess of Democracy, and all of that is in the eyes of the Chinese woman in the kitchen of the Hotel Bela Vista in Macao, which crumbles and decays and disintegrates, the last remnant of Portugal, the last remnant of Europe, in front of whose entrance not the heat of Macao spreads out but the Square of Heavenly Peace with the potato peelings that now even hang out of the windows of the gambling casino of Macao, that heap upon the gambling tables and cover the green and yellow felt, that become drunken in the red felt puddles with a fluid that comes from the interior part of the potatoes. They're no longer playing with chips, but with potato peelings, with soaked potato peelings, many of which still cling to the bayonets and cannot be scraped off, as they stick stubbornly to the boots of soldiers, to heels, toes, and soles, to the hands of soldiers, the barrels of rifles, clubs, to tanks, and as finally they bring the blades of army helicopters to a stop, because they won't turn anymore because of all the potato peelings.

A person was run over by a tank as by a train. And the spine was twisted in a grotesque way, as though someone had tried to turn it into a spiral.

He goes on until I am on the beach.

The beach is lonely and empty.

For a time the professor leans tilted against a wall and looks into the sky.

Then I discover a young girl who walks along the edge of the waves.

He observes the adolescent child, but is ignored by her.

The girl pulls a letter from a pocket, reads it, lets her arms fall.

Now the girl raises her arms again, reads the letter once more, rips it into little pieces, folds the pieces again and again, rips them once more, finally throws the paper scraps into the air. They return like confetti.

The wind carries them like birds into the surf.

Butterflies of oblivion.

The girl stands there, looking into the water.

For a long time she stands that way, until she takes a handkerchief out of her skirt pocket.

The professor thinks he notices that the child sobs. I hear her crying.

The wind blows into the girl's face.

I turn away.

He hides his face against the wall.

And he thinks of the letters that he has written and never mailed.

No letter will leave Macao, no card, not a word.

There will be no one who will try to catch the butterflies of oblivion.

Finally, he turns away from the wall, walks a short distance, looks over the wall.

A child's ball, from which the air has escaped, lies there.

Father, explain grass to me.

But instead there was the little treasure chest of paternal maxims for upbringing.

No laws for the righteous, no advice for the wise.

Beware of being victorious over superiors.

Knowledge is long, life is short, and whoever knows nothing is also not alive.

A mediocre head will get farther with zeal than a headless smart man.

Things splendid are few and seldom.

Whoever turns the tiger loose must also be able to ride it.

Stand within earshot of kindness.

Think like the least and speak like the most.

Consider the outcome when you move into the house of good fortune.

Art in enterprise, circumspection in inquiry.

Empty nothing to the dregs.

Have the right stomach for a big bite.

Make it possible to be wished back.

He isn't stupid who does something stupid, unless he doesn't know how to cover it up.

Never consort with someone who will put you in the shade.

Never tell the whole truth without lying.

Undertake something easy as though it were difficult, something difficult as though it were easy.

Don't appear to be effective, be so.

Be more than you appear to be.

Whoever cannot don a lion skin, my son, should wear a fox pelt.

Be able to wait until grass has grown over the matter.

Father, tell me what grass is.

Tell me, please, why grass always has to grow over something.

Father, tell me what lies under the grass.

Father, tell me what grass is.

Father, when we go walking on Sunday and I hold your hand and we have to greet all the people, then do tell me, pretty please, what grass is.

Father, has grass also grown over the one to whom you tipped your hat, or, Father, did he scatter grass on your head?

Father, tell me what grass is.

And why couldn't my father ever explain grass to me?

Because he was interested only in the concrete that he poured over the grass. He got rich manufacturing precision instruments such as compasses and gauges, particularly like those urgently needed by Hitler's general staff.

The secret passion of my father was, however, the autobahns. He always believed Adolf Hitler was the inventor of the autobahn because even during his Landsberg incarceration he thought about the construction of roads without intersections.

My father knew marvelous words:

AVUS and STUFA, HAFRABA and MULEIBERL, LEHA, STUFISTRA and GEZUVOR.

On the Sunday afternoon strolls he explained all of them to me, and I had to recite them like a poem.

STUFA: Society for the Technical Undertaking for Autobahns

HAFRABA: The Society for the Groundwork of the Highway Hansa-Cities–Frankfurt–Basle

MULEIBERL: Munich–Leipzig–Berlin

LEHA: Leipzig–Halle

GEZUVOR: Group Effort Zuider Zee: Variation on Reconstruction

My father was a member.

Instead of telling me about grass, he always talked only about turning the first sod and raved about Dr. Todt's plans for an Avenue of Peace. My father didn't want to think about the boots of soldiers on that avenue, rather Nordic men and vehicles.

My father admired Dr. Fritz Todt, the engineer, and on Sunday afternoon I had to repeat who that was: SS-Unit Commander and Major-General of the Luftwaffe, Reich Minister for Armament and Munitions, Commanding General for the Regulation of Agriculture, Inspector General for the German Road System, Inspector General for Water and Energy, full professor, head of the Main Office for Technology and Reich Administrator of the National Socialist League of German Technology, to which Father also belonged.

Many sentences of my father began with the words: Dr. Todt said...

Dr. Todt said: "Whoever tries to solve material questions only from a material side succumbs to matter. Only he who overcomes it with his spirit will become master of matter."

My father told me that, but not about the grass.

With the autobahns my father built my grandfather's precision-tool shop into an enterprise. With Hitler's autobahns my father became wealthy. Compasses and measuring tools were later manufactured only in branch factories or in work at home. Only Dr. Todt's mysterious plane crash after a visit to the Führer's headquarters on the 7th of February 1942 caused my father to be disconcerted. But it was already too late. He who arrives too late is punished by history, my father said. And instead of telling me about grass, he recited his favorite poem about the Reich autobahn: *Do you see the ribbon of the long road winding? Bring on the gravel! We pound the asphalt. The iron axles of the roller grinding. On both sides stand the green woods at a halt. The mixers all the gray disks turning. Hark, a thrush sings its song in the wood. We may not stay on this spot yearning because the road keeps going on along. The roller has already crushed the stones—brightly glows the fast-rolled ribbon of the band. We drive it on, are driven by its tones. It strives from town to city, from ocean onto land. Along through fields, where high the blades are waving, past woods and meadow, quarry and acres of farm, on through valleys, high over arched bridges paving, our road draws a broadly branched arm. Now leave the rollers, leave the gray truck rotors. A work arose from earth and steel and stone. The road sings in the chugging of the motors. A monument our labor will atone.*

But over it all my father thought up an orderly mind that spoke from a cloud of gunpowder.

That's what our Sunday strolls were about.

But only the grass, he never told me about the grass.

But it is written: Honor thy father and thy mother, that thy days may be long in the land that Jehovah thy God giveth thee.

Dear Mother Mary,

Ever since I can remember, you sit suffering in your chair at the window in your convent. You have taken leave of time, retreated into your grief, and begun to write your own calendar. You have never been interested in me or my work, your memories of your firstborn have let all else become second-rate.

You have never asked me how I spend my days and my nights, what I busy myself with, what devours my time, and when you said the word *professor*, it always sounded a bit contemptuous.

Last summer I happened to speak in my lecture about the unknown Portuguese poet João de Araujo Coreia. He was a doctor and was born the same year as father. In his *Contos Bárbados* he tells a story that could be your story. You never neglected letting me feel how much you're convinced that my work represents only flight into the make-believe reality of books, has nothing to do with real life and nothing with our family.

Coreia's story can prove the opposite to you, and therefore I will translate it for you.

Imagine a mother, a widow with two sons.

One son is considered, from the time he could walk, to be a do-nothing. No one is able to follow his odd fantasy; he plays all kinds of pranks, most of which end badly; he crouches in the damage. Finally the fifteen-year-old devil is shunted off on relatives in Brazil. His mother never heard anything of him again and was not exactly unhappy about that. But the other child is a sweet baby with the face of an angel and a glowing sign on his forehead that makes his mother certain, for only she sees it, that something special will come of this child some day. Fate has something immense in store for him.

When he is five the boy is already attending school and, soon after, the teacher says that there's nothing more he can teach him. Do you remember, Mother, how old I was when I was sent to school and how horribly I suffered from it? Instead of playing with other children, the divine son collects miniatures of saints and becomes an altar boy. Sometimes he fasts, too, and his snow-white hands become even thinner. No sooner is he allowed to go to confession than he misses no opportunity to confess his childish sins. Then his mother makes her decision: Her son shall become a canon. When did you decide, Mother, to make a priest of me, an ordained gentleman, as you always said? When did you get the idea of buying your place in eternity with me? Comprehensive insurance, for you would have been best satisfied if I had become a priest and my brother a head medical doctor in a hospital, while father longed for a banker or a finance minister. But you wanted a direct wire to God. Do you recall how I laid the tablecloth about my shoulders, set up candles, and celebrated high mass? You stood by with expectant, gleaming eyes. Admit it, admit it at least for once. The mother furthers the ambitions of the boy. She lets him get through the fifth grade and then sends him to secondary school, where Latin is studied from the start. The language of the gods. From sunup to sunset the mother hardly eats because she must think of the Latin words and of her place at the right hand of God. But the boy reaches puberty, glances furtively at skirts, and begins to be indolent. He yawns more times than there are beads on a rosary. And he pollutes his bed. Already his scholarly accomplishments become catastrophic; his mother talks to his teachers and carries a riding crop under her coat. She wants to cure her son from putting his hands under his blankets. Several such years must be endured. While the boy burgeons and the girls also turn to him, his mother becomes hardened. She hardens as though she were sitting in a wheelchair at the window of an elegant convent, mourning her blessed firstborn, who shortly after the war—what a misfortune—played with a hand grenade and blew out the light of his young life, as her spiritual adviser used to express it. The mother's face became gloomy, her hands are as dried out as her lips, through which come now only prayers. They never kissed again, but they force the boy to sit over his books until late at night, to eat dry bread, to resist the tempter, to become a bishop. If you crave white grapes, eat black ones.

In those years his mother teaches him that, and the boy with the face of an angel and the sign on his brow becomes something hard. After his splendid degree summa cum laude, the youth enrolls in the School of Theology at the Catholic University. Even his life as a student doesn't get him offtrack. He goes along, even—as they say—sows his wild oats, leaves his dormitory and the prefect to go to lectures, returns to review the lectures. He seldom finds his way in summer to the river meadows and even then, with his books. His first mass is celebrated in grand style, his priestly blessing fully savored. And already his rise in the form of red stockings and cummerbund is enticing. The priestly gentleman has himself photographed in a seraphic pose: for his mother's dressing table. What a handsome man. He writes to his mother and implores her to move in with him. But you decline, you decline without a word, Mother, while in his mind he sees you sitting in his salon, taciturn and dressed in black. The gentleman is transferred to the capital and promoted. He is active as a decorative prelate, marries blue-blooded wedding pairs, baptizes lucky children, participates in scientific, even more in benevolent conferences, occasionally even takes the dignified post of presider, lets ladies persuade him to accept particularly discreet invitations to parties. No woman dares wear a too deeply cut gown in his presence. They practice secretly only before their domestic mirror. The prelate is exemplary for his polished speech, his fine manners: in the midst of countesses, a prince of the blood. Although a man of the world, he forgets neither conscientious practice of devotions nor compassion. No one more fervently prays and turns his gaze away from temptation and toward Heaven.

So, you like that, Mother, that's what you had in mind and wished for.

Already the staff of a bishop is offered him, already he is transferred to another city, where he begins immediately to establish an aura of worldly splendor. He assembles the best musicians and cooks about him, society opens its doors to him, moreover a few courses are completed at the university; he is a great patron of the arts and is skilled in serene good manners. He is a man, say the initiated, who brings to life the good old times of the princely bishops. His voice carries weight; what he doesn't want doesn't happen.

That's what you wanted, my Mother, that's what you dreamed, admit it.

The prince sees through malicious and ambitious men and gives them no chance. To make up for that he does good deeds for the poor. But his mother continues to wear herself out on her quest, even more than she needed to, because it has become habit for her. The sweets that her son has sent her she lets go bad. The way you have done with all the gifts, Mother, that I sent to the convent for you. His mother becomes as avaricious as hunger itself.

But since the years pass by for all men, the mother feels more and more weary and exhausted.

Again the son gets it into his head to take his mother into his house. He chooses a nun with a sense for tact, a power of empathy, and with the best upbringing to look after his mother, of whom he speaks now only as his Lady Mother.

Everything happens in accordance with his will, but after only a week you write me: "See to it that this woman leaves the house at once, or I will wring her neck as one does chickens'."

What chance would I have had as a bishop against such maternal words, Mother? From now on you receive my favors merely feebly and say: "Even stones are worshipped for the sake of saints." You're making my life a hell. The star of the princely bishop is sinking, at first barely noticeably, finally in the sight of all. Soon better society, which has the say, will want to have nothing to do with him. They will avoid him, cut him, ridicule him and his silly mother-love in the press. The name of the bishop will disappear, and no one would have been surprised if one day it were said of him that he had been stabbed at night on a public street or that he had died in prison.

And of that mother the poet Correia writes, dear Mother: "She had treated her son worse than a bitch dog would have."

But what did the mother do?

She longed for her potatoes; one day took up the hoe and began to tear the grass out of the bishop's beds and to turn over the soil. Then she took seeds out of her apron pocket and scattered them into the loosened soil at intervals that she measured with the width of her hand, panting with satisfaction. But her smile was as pale as the candles that burned on the altar. Singing, she went back into her house, lighted the fire, cooked herself a potato soup, ate it with relish, and warmed her scrawny body in front of the biggest fire that she had ever kindled in her life.

Dear Mother,

You are sitting in your chair at the window in your convent. Do you know where your chair stands, within which walls, with which view? Your convent was not always a convent.

Once upon a time there was an institution that earlier had a different name.

Once upon a time there was an institution that earlier was once a nursing home.

Once upon a time there was a nursing-care home in which neither nursing nor care were practiced.

There was killing there.

So-called "things unfit to live" were killed there by pious nuns and upright helpers, approved by priests, in plain sight.

Even you must have known about it, Mother.

Today you believe you can erase the past by staying in the same institution that once had a different name.

Untruthful letters were written from the institution.

"We regret to have to inform you that Mr./Mrs./Miss… died of tuberculosis today, the…, at… o'clock. Since our institution is specified only as a transit institution for such sick people who should be transferred to another institution in our region and their stay here serves solely to identify bearers of the bacillus that is, as is well known, always found among such sick people, the responsible police authorities have ordered protective measures and, in accordance with Paragraph 22 of the Code to Control Contagious Diseases, have decreed the cremation of the body and the disinfection of belongings. A declaration of consent is not required in this case. Since the deceased wore only institutional clothing, personal belongings do not exist. In the event that you wish to bury the urn in a particular cemetery, you will bear the costs of transfer. Enclosed are two copies of the death certificate for official submission. *Heil* Hitler!"

Many a corpse lay there as though run over by a train, and the spine was twisted in a grotesque way as though a great force had tried to turn it into a spiral.

Dear Mother,

More than a hundred such letters were sent from your convent, and in the mathematics textbook from the year of my birth was the following problem: "The construction of an asylum for the insane requires six million Reichsmarks. How many settlements at 15,000 Reichsmarks apiece could have been built for that?" Where you sit at the window, Mother, the worthless consumers were lodged, whose destruction was a natural law and thus the will of God, as the pious called it. Even a film was made in your convent, in which the most serious cases were shown: behind bars. And from all over Bavaria the mayors were carried to Irsee, to show them the expensive façade and let them see the waste of tax monies. Did you never hear anything about the *Mercy Death Campaign*; did you know nothing about the strips of adhesive tape that were stuck to the backs of the doomed before they were driven by the *Cooperative Society for the Transport of the Sick* in curtained buses and with armed escorts to the gas chambers? How do you like the view, Mother? You look across at a small grove, with comfortable benches to rest on, and lovely walkways. Underneath them lie the buried, Mother. And when I asked: Father, tell me about the grass, he couldn't tell me. And you, too, never told me about the grass. Since the transfer campaigns had been known by the public, in your convent the starvation method was then employed. For this purpose special squads were set up in which only the so-called D-rations (D for deprivation) were allowed to be distributed: a ration without vitamins and fat. The campaign was begun in the Irsee Convent in August of 1942. Cause of death: edema from malnutrition. The director of the institution gave politically racist speeches and was a member of the *Reich Committee for the Scientific Survey of Serious Ailments Conditioned by Heredity and Tendency*. He successfully supported the establishment of pediatric departments. Many parents thanked him in moving letters for his devoted care. They never saw how, after the lethal injection, the skin of their children turned green as though verdigris were sprouting even in the corners of their mouths. Since the cemetery of your convent, dear Mother, soon became too small and even in the grove no more corpses could be buried, a crematory was built with an oven of the latest design, with vaulted coffin chambers and an ash collector. The Thulsian craftsmen worked quickly and well: within six weeks the installation was ready to operate. And when the Americans arrived, they didn't dare enter your convent, Mother, because outside of it a sign hung with the inscription: *Typhus*. But the chief surgeon had given himself and his daughter lethal injections. And the crematorium was long since torn down by the thorough Thulsian craftsmen who again earned money on it.

Once upon a time there was a convent that earlier claimed to have been a nursing-care home.

Once upon a time there was an eight-hundred-year anniversary celebration of the Irsee Convent.

Once upon a time there was a commemorative volume.

Once upon a time there was a Mercy Death Campaign.

Once upon a time there was a commemorative volume in which that chapter is missing. Mothers sit quietly and reproachfully in their chairs at the windows overlooking the park and sing the beautiful song "Onceuponatime." For a long time they have not known what goes on in the world outside the gates of their convent, for they have transferred the world into the convent, and that's enough for them.

Outside, the seed is sprouting, dear Mother.

The ghosts appear even in daylight.

They stopped observing the agreed-upon hour a long time ago.

If one child goes, the mothers console themselves easily with the next one.

After all, there was always my brother.

And he was born before me and had a more affable nature.

If the gods take one son, dear Mother, then they send another.

Even in his sandbox my brother is said to have liked building bridges. At least that's what family legend claims. And when he watched over me in the sandbox because he was older, I am said to have liked to destroy his bridges, as legend claims. And because it makes that claim, it's probably true. In any case, I can't remember. I remember only the legend. At first it was told affectionately; later, reproaches crept in. After we had quarreled frequently and thoroughly enough and fallen out with one another, my brother and I hardly conversed. Our meetings were limited to courteous visits to our parents' home. There we tried to preserve appearances and get along with one another, but in reality we never got along. We merely pretended to. At the parental coffee table my brother loved to talk about his bridges. He talked about the idea of connection and about the idea of understanding, called bridges more important than houses and holier than cathedrals, talked about overcoming natural obstructions, brought harmony and exchange, trade and change, traffic and philosophy into play, wanted to make up and unite over bridges, wanted to know that separations were suspended, and in all earnestness was of the opinion that all our hopes always lay on the other side, just as a neighbor's cherries were sweeter, and to get there, bridges were necessary. He became totally unbearable when he gave his lecture on *Streuselkuchen*. His almond-topped cake seminars. While the family devoured tarts and shoveled whipped cream, it had to put up with being taught about the spirit of invention and the assertive will of pontifices, pretend to be interested in primitive girder bridges and suspension bridges; it learned about Mandrokles of Samos and his pontoon bridges, was told about the Danube bridge of Apollodoros of Damascus, which was patterned on the Trajan Column in Rome. The family was hounded over the aqueduct of Segovia, by the Ponte Vecchio and through all the jewelry shops on its shoulders, sighed about the Rialto Bridge, about wooden, iron, and steel constructions, about reinforced concrete and suspension bridges; talk was of Thomas Telford, who herded sheep in Scotland before he spanned the Menai Road in Wales; there was raving about the carpenter brothers Grubenmann from Teufen in the Swiss canton of Appenzell, about the *frères pontiffes*, the order of bridge builders of Saint Jacques du Maupas, *sur le* Pont d'Avignon, and again and again my brother had to talk about his attempts to improve nature with his extravagances and about his childish search for the removal of separations because all our hopes always lay on the other side and so on and so on.

My brother's childhood play-bridges.

Brother: I am a bridge.

Me: I don't want to be a bridge.

Brother: Everyone is a bridge.

Me: Except me.

Brother: I lie over an abyss.

Me: I am a rushing river.

Brother: I have bitten into your banks.

Me: I wash around you, but you are not up to my power.

Brother: I wait to connect both banks.

Me: You are waiting to collapse.

Brother: I hear steps, the creaking of wheels, people.

Me: That is the cracking of your pillars.

Brother: I stretch, for my pillars are flexible.

Me: They won't endure.

Brother: No bridge once built can stop being a bridge without collapsing.

Me: You can no longer bear the load; it's getting too much for you.

Brother: I can bear anything if only I want to, for there are supporting pillars.

Me: It's not a question of construction.

Brother: Statics must be right, the theory of the equilibrium of forces, of the condition of tension and displacement of the supporting structure.

Me: The opposite of static is dynamic. It sounds like dynamite.

Brother: I am a staticist.

Me: Father knows how to handle dynamite.

Brother: Father has never handled dynamite.

Me: Father blew up bridges during the war.

Brother: Did Father say that?

Me: The grass that grew over the subject told me.

Brother: Did Father finally tell you about the grass?

Me: He was able to tell me.

Brother: A bridge always knows two sides.

Me: A bridge without a memory isn't worth anything. It will collapse at the slightest weight. A clump of grass is enough.

My dear brother, do you know about the construction of the great Thulsian bridge? The construction engineer had promised to finish the bridge by a specific date. When it was approaching, he saw that it was impossible to keep his promise. When only two days remained until the due date, he called up the Devil and asked him for assistance. The Devil appeared and offered to finish the bridge himself during the last night, if the construction engineer would deliver to him the first living creature that crossed it. The pact was signed, and during the last night, without a single human eye being able to see what was happening in the darkness, the Devil finished building the bridge. At the break of dawn the construction engineer came, driving a rooster across the bridge before him, and handed it over to the Devil. But the latter had desired a human soul, and when he saw himself deceived, he angrily grabbed the rooster, tore it to pieces, and threw it through the bridge, from which came the two holes that even to this day cannot be cemented shut because at night everything falls apart that is done on it during the day. And now tell me, my revered brother, where are your statics now? Whoever blocks a bridge with bars will find himself behind bars. I know the secret of your statics, because it is the secret of all bridge builders through the ages: They always walled in children for the propitiation of the river deity and the safety of the construction.

Again and again walled in children and, to strengthen the mortar, added blood. Sir, some day the great Bridge Day of Judgment will come. I will inaugurate it with the following words: *March across, march across, across the bridge of gold. It is in two, it is in two, but we will fix it up with little stones and little bones, the last to cross must pay, we're told.*

My brother's greatest joy is to build the golden bridge. It must be massive and solid, if it is to fulfill its purpose: to lead across something that was thought to be impassable. We trust hardly anyone more than we do a bridge builder. Can we imagine a pessimistic bridge builder? He wants it daring but safe. He trusts his instincts for weight characteristics, his power of empathy in weight ratios. With bridges the weight-bearing and -supporting members must be mighty and strong; what is suspended must be hovering and easily measured, he says.

My brother builds bridges from which I will plunge. Every pillar that he sets, every bold arch that he spans will serve me as a ramp. The more daring the construction, the deadlier the fall. My brother knows what he's doing. The idea of bringing together is no good, unless the renewed parting is possible. To demonstrate that parting is my grandest task.

That's why I must plunge into the depths.

My brother is forcing that duty on me.

He never asked Father to tell him about the

grass, for he knew the secret from the moment he was born.

Presumably my brother bundled me up, set me on the bicycle, and told me about the trees and the birds.

But he didn't want to tell me about the grass.

For when I was a child he walled me into his bridges.

He always showed a family sense for that.

He knows something about skiing, about cars, and soccer. Besides he is congenial, and he's always obliging.

Righteous also in his anger.

Successful in his profession.

Everyone can see what he does.

He builds bridges all over the world.

What could a professor of Lusitanics offer of any value?

Only once did I visit my brother, and stood beside him at the window. Fog hung over the roofs, the shapes of the antennas split apart a yellow-green sky; somewhere a locomotive whistled; in the neighborhood a radio bawled the hit of the summer: *If you don't know me by now.*

My brother sighed.

Behind his back his two daughters were scuffling and making all kinds of demands. Now they wanted this bought, now that. My sister-in-law, for a change bustling about in the kitchen, scolds her children, but doing so has my brother in mind.

I looked out the window. On the street below a girl with a short skirt and wild hair was walking past.

My brother commented: "Maybe soon I'll get very old," and I replied: "Just imagine that these are the last moments of your life. Remember them: the sky, the whistle of the locomotive, the antennas, the fog, the music, and the girl down there."

We got no farther than that because his daughters called for their father to overwhelm him with questions to which he had no answer. My brother withdrew into his study, looked for documents but found only a newspaper behind which he would have liked to hide himself. But his daughters went on romping in his study and chanted litanies of things they wanted to have, had to have, absolutely and on the spot. Something flew through the room. Maybe a red ball. A glass bowl was swept off the desk and broke into pieces. My brother put his newspaper aside and said:

"No one has the right to intrude into my dreams," and spoke again of building bridges.

I imagine what night would be like: How his wife would pester him with new demands and goad him to make more money, to become even more successful and famous. I heard her weep with disappointment and watched my brother lying there, his arms crossed behind his neck. Soon he would again travel abroad to conclude new contracts. Out of jealousy his wife bit him on the arm.

Suddenly quiet prevailed in the room. The children had disappeared, there was a smell of printer's ink. My brother was standing at the window and did not react to the ringing of the telephone. He turned and stared at a corner. Over the roofs fog hung; the shapes of antennas broke up a yellow-green sky; somewhere a locomotive whistled; in the neighborhood a radio bawled. My brother propped his elbows against the window. Below, a girl with a short skirt and wild hair passed by.

I had died, and my brother had to get my body released. I lay there, and my spine was twisted in a grotesque way, as though a great force had tried to turn it in a spiral. From my deathbed I see him arrive at the hospital; while he takes care of the formalities I look over his shoulder. Precise and composed, he receives expressions of condolence. Finally he appears in the death room and surrenders to his distress. Surreptitiously he wipes a tear from his cheek. Then he gives a sign to the men from the undertaker. They bed me in a casket and nail me in. Carefully they roll me to the elevator at the rear entrance. A horse-drawn vehicle awaits below. The men lift me onto the wagon, heave the casket with a crack onto the wagon bed. My brother slips out of his elegant black needlepoint. Underneath he wears the coarse cloth of a coachman. He pays the men, just gives them a couple of bills. He swings himself up onto the coach box, snorts, lifts the reins, slaps them on the back of the horse, the wagon starts with a lurch. The men from the undertaker spit into their hands and look after the cart. My brother turns again on the coach box, waves back with the whip, urges the horse into a gallop. The trip crosses the fields through the beautiful land of Thulsern. We stop at every tavern. Each time my brother climbs down from the box, orders a boy to look after his nag, enters the tavern, and starts drinking. He grabs at the bodices of the waitresses, devours platters of meat, lingers for card games and old-timers' political discussions before he careens outside again, swings himself up onto the box to click his tongue and slap the reins on the horse's back. My brother gets drunker and drunker. He can't leave out a single tavern. For a long time now we've been driving into the night; we got lost a long time ago. So my brother drives overland with me. For days, for nights. Finally we reach a bridge that my brother built. He stops, wrestles the coffin from the wagon bed. It costs him some effort before he can topple it over the balustrade into the depths below. Or: Every Sunday my brother will visit the grave. He'll always come at the same time: late afternoon. Whenever he's late, he'll excuse himself long-windedly. Stony-faced he'll stand there sewed into his suit, his hands crossed over his crotch; he'll stare at the inscription on the gravestone before he bends over to pluck at the small plants, scrape a little bit in the dirt, or collect the leaves that the wind has blown over. Fresh flowers will always be provided, even in the winter. From the cemetery rise my brother will gaze silently over the countryside. Sometimes there'll be a distant sound in the air, but perhaps he'll only imagine that, when he'll clatter the watering can or set it down on the grave enclosure. Ivy and clematis will climb around the gravestone, on which the letters will gradually become weathered, until one day my name will have disappeared completely. But even then my brother will stand at my grave and be silent, as he was silent through all the years, and will turn his hat in his hands in embarrassment. My brother will consider how he'll be able to build a bridge into eternity, and he'll want to speak with me about his plan. But not a word will cross his lips.

Still, I'll know exactly what he wants to say to me.

His life will not suffice to tell about it.

Just as my life will not suffice to recover from my parting from Mary.

Dearest Mary,

day of my night, glory of my pain, polar star of my way, guiding star of my good fortune, as Don Quixote would have put it. He knows who Dulcinea really is: the farm girl Aldonza Lorenzo, who Sancho Panza says is as strong as a bull, dirty, can bawl at the peasants from the church tower and be heard for miles, knows about all kinds of teases, and besides has something about her of a whore. The knight knows all that—and still he pays honor to her as the noblest of princesses. And he loves her. And because he loves her, he raises her up and makes her incomparable, singular, when he says: "The question of status is of no consequence. I shape her in my fantasy, as I desire her. And let the world think what it will." Don Quixote's sense of justice can be realized only through love. The letters that he addressed to his adored one are proof of that: "All-governing, sublime Lady! The one thrust through with the point of the sword of separation, the one pierced to his innermost heart with pain wishes for you the well-being that he himself does not have." And he signs with: "Yours until death, The Knight of the Woeful Countenance." In life such love is not possible. So it must be invented. Or, to put it in the words of my ideal: "Do you believe that the Amaryllises, the Phyllises, the Sylvias, the Dianas, the Galatheas, the Filidas, and the rest of those with whom books, romances, barbershops, comedy stages are filled were really ladies of flesh and blood and really the beloveds of those who exalted them? Of course not; rather they fabricated most of them to create objects for their verses and to be valid for youths glowing with love and for those who are worthy of love. And so it suffices for me that I think and believe that the exquisite Aldonza Lorenzo is beautiful...."

Dearest Mary, it cannot be chance that we became acquainted in Toboso on the occasion of an excursion that I made there with my students. It was in Toboso—do you remember?—and you said to me, Maria Dolores, Maria Dolorosa, Niña Maria Almayer, that you were a Toledana, with the first name of my mother, a woman from the city of superior swords and poisoned rapiers.

You, Mary, you are my Dulcinea. And you, too, are nothing more than an invention of my longing for a love that here below is neither livable nor lovable. But should you, in the letters I have not sent you, recognize yourself, then you have let yourself be deceived by your mirrored image. It is not of this world. It comes from a better one.

It comes from the world of books. Just as Dulcinea is a sketch by Quixote, I am a hasty sketch by you, Mary.

Most beloved, what are you doing just now? Are you washing socks or are you sitting in front of the television set, have you gone to the movies for a sad, beautiful film, or are you in love just now with a man, have you become happy? Do you still know how it was when there were no frontiers for us in our illusion, yes, it was an illusion. But there is no greater truth than that of illusion, and how bitter it is when such illusions burst; but believe me, they may not wish to become reality, for otherwise they would die and would erase the memory of them that is at least as precious as the illusion itself. Just imagine that we really experienced all that, we lived it and were blissful doing so because we did not know that we must part and that nothing can be enduring, and we are completely desperate about it because we don't wish to realize that there can be no fulfillment in love, never ever. Love appears as a fiction of fiction, and with that the ground reels beneath our feet. But just imagine—I have, after your all-emaciating reproach—that Don Quixote claimed with mind and soul that place that belongs to you, to you alone, and that's why you returned to Toledo. I do not know the whys and wherefores of why he enchanted me more than you and your thousand moods, I do not know—I have again begun to read the Stoics, for it is not only vexing and tiresome to fret about something that's beyond my power, rather more than that it's senseless and stupid, and in this way I thought I could set out on the path to *apatheia*, to a dispassionate state; the old Stoic ideal of the renunciation of the world seemed to me a proven remedy against pain; but I lack the faith in a divine order, and so *autarkia*, *ataraxia*, and *apatheia* remained, in the final analysis, only empty words; they did not seem suitable as cardinal virtues for my requirements, for until now there has been no philosopher who was able to bear toothache with patience, even if the wise man was on the same footing with the gods, cheerful, peaceful, and filled with joy. So at best I could agree with Seneca, when reading him I found: "All men are deluded by deceptive and brief diversions that pay the cheerful mania of a single hour with long-enduring revulsion, such as applause and noisy agreement that have been achieved with great excitement and must be atoned for." Following Seneca's advice I avoided crowds. Why a suit of armor? Why swordplay? All that simply postpones death. With these lines I began to understand how short the step is from the Stoics to rat poison. Let's thank God that no one can be kept alive. But it couldn't be a suicide from the balcony, nor did I want to hang my corpse in your room, Mary, for if I behaved that way, then I would not be seeking death but its effect on the living that I would like to have experienced along with them. So it could not be. A bit later I began to excerpt Epictetus' conversations and carry scraps of paper in my wallet.

I'll give you an example: "Of things that are present, some are in our power and others not. The happiness of a man and his peace of mind depend on his concerning himself only with things that are in his power and on his learning to leave those things alone that are not in his power." Of course, doing that I had to get rid of the thought of my love for you, because it is not in my power.

Earlier he had sometimes wondered why events did not come to those who waited for them. Now he tried to ban them from the most sensitive corner of his heart. Mary's return home to Toledo had made him into someone who turned at night to the shadow on the wall, in order to think up silly and marvelous things that were lured out by the pangs of jealousy. Every day this old man seemed to distance himself from his not-so-old life; every day he understood it less. What did it have to do with him anyway? To live in disappointment meant for him to live without illusions. He had succumbed to the greatest illusion under the sun. All is in vain, he kept saying to himself, and one must at least have the courage to have no pretenses. He no longer saw a chance to extend his own possibilities in the clashes of the impossible and the possible. Was it exhaustion that brought such a consideration to him? The challenge and the confidence that he had hurled at life as a young man were used up. As though water had swallowed them up like shipwrecked people. Now he felt that his life was nothing more than the passage of particles of time and supposed success: even in regard to Mary. One scrap after another floated past him, and his hours dragged along and became more and more indifferent to him. It was past, Mary had gone. On a Thursday.

In our imagination we still exchanged letters in which the words no longer knew how far they could go. When it is difficult to love, then it is clear whether one is serious or not. The times when we blocked our paths with gifts already slid into our memory. And then her image again: quite near. Her hair as black as the wing of a crow. Her smile, which shows how little it costs to despise a loser. Slowly the scream rose from his abdomen, but when it lay on his tongue, it wouldn't come out. Someone who was once me, with the feeling of letting myself fall into a well.

Do you remember my promise, Mary, one day to travel across the sea in a train. Do you remember? My promise was embedded so deeply inside me that I took it with my dreams. They were such old dreams, such as perhaps are dreamed only by trees. And in dreams I sat with you in an elegant compartment, and we slowly left the city, and you were laughing. We traveled ever farther on that train—which rolled like a ship—and overcome with happiness did not want to return to shore. But in the middle of the ocean it began to pitch. At first I laughed with you, but then its pitching became so wild that I fell out of the compartment. A ridiculous figure. But the train traveled on toward shore with you. I quickened my swimming strokes, but I knew that I would never ever catch up with you. You paused and turned the train. Finally you were coming toward me. You came nearer, laughing. I was relieved. I was about to reach my hands toward you when the train moved faster, finally caught me, and rolled on over me until I slowly sank. I lay in a compartment, and my spine was twisted in a grotesque way as though a great force had tried to turn it in a spiral.

Love, when it ends, is a lonely affair of empty words and formalities. A ritual made its way in stereotypical spirals; the duel became a shadow play; words of love were spooled onto an endless spool and disguised themselves as words of parting. The lovers who parted soon became voyeurs in their own house of mirrors. It was no consolation to him when he tried to tell himself that in the final analysis all women and girls were the same. Neither was the image consoling of one morning awakening no longer beside his beloved but next to a woman named Mary, who was his mother. He sought flight in aphorisms that led him to believe that love was something too wonderful for one to be allowed to waste time with the fate of two persons whose only merit was to possess it, even though in an inexplicable way. Early, much too early, the lies had begun. And he had lied most loathsomely, because he always tried to tell the truth in order to disguise the soul of facts. Perhaps he had begun right there to lose Mary. Now he had become so vulnerable that he feared that every raindrop could kill him. Now he understood how ridiculous love can be. Is there anything more ridiculous than a languishing lover who sits in front of a telephone and waits for a word, for a syllable, for the breath of a woman he loves? Already he saw her lying in the arms of another, already he imagined, just now, at this very moment, that they were doing it together and laughing at him, rightly so, because in his jealousy he was acting like an idiot, more ridiculous than a schoolboy.

Ridiculous.

Ridiculous, so many feelings; ridiculous, to have had and have wasted so many hopes; ridiculous, finally, this pose of the abandoned lover who still had not understood that it was over and past; ridiculous that he involved me particularly. But it involves not only me, it involves thousands daily; without fail someone is abandoned, although he loves, because he loves, because love knows no mercy, rather only the enchantment of the beginning when feelings are cloudy and reason is sent on vacation. The beginning is always enchanting, head-turning, ardent, anything you want you can have, and even much more, and all at once, nothing tolerates postponement, it must be now and on the spot: whether it makes any sense or not. There is no question of after, no more than of mercy and forgiveness after a ridiculous defeat. Every breath after a foundered love tells what open eyes recognize as painfully clear in the darkness.

I see a girl take a letter out of her pocket. She

reads the letter, then tears it into little pieces, folding the bits again and again, ripping them once more, finally throwing the paper scraps into the air. They fall like confetti.

The wind carries them like birds into the surf.

3

Squashing Birds

All is in vain, and one must at least have the courage to have no pretenses.

I was taught what that means by an old Portuguese, whom I looked up a few years ago. No one I asked knew the man, about whom I knew only that he lived as an ear, nose, and throat doctor in Coimbra. In the lower city. And I knew his name: Rocha. To meet this man, by whom I had read only a few sentences in out-of-print books, I traveled to Coimbra. I had to see him.

When I asked the bellboy cautiously about Rocha, astonishment crossed his face. Yes indeed, he knew Rocha, an important man. Of course, every child in Coimbra knew Rocha. What a question! At once the bellboy left my suitcase standing, turned around, took me by the hand as though I were a blind man, and led me out of the hotel, across the intersection, and pointed at a crumbling façade. The bellboy ignored a red light—he was suddenly in a hurry, as though Rocha could not endure a postponement. A long index finger pointed at a sign: Adolfo Rocha, Medico Especialista, Ouvidos, Nariz e Garganta. Suddenly I was standing alone at the building entrance; the bellboy had disappeared. Inside and up dark stairs to the second floor. Gingerly I knocked, the door was ajar. I entered a modest waiting room that looked as though it were anticipating a furniture mover, to be emptied at any moment. A clearing of my throat, a cough, nothing. Rocha is not here. But then the door to the examining room opened and in the door frame appeared—completely unreal with the light in my eyes—a very tall, slender, handsome old man. He stood wearing his smock and asked softly but energetically what I wanted.

I explained. In front of me stands Rocha in his doctor's smock, with a slightly amused expression on his face. The old man asks me to come on in. His examining room is even smaller than his waiting room. At the window I see a small desk hopelessly overflowing with manuscripts. Embarrassed among them stands an antediluvian typewriter. Next to the door, on an examining table, lies a mountain of boxes of medications, covered by a thick layer of dust.

Rocha offers me no seat. Neither does he sit down, rather he leans at an angle against the wall, parallel to the slant of the afternoon sun. Slowly the man begins to speak. His slender hands narrate. The afternoon becomes warily older, but Rocha does not sit down, and I, too, stand, but only out of respect, although I am dog-tired from my trip. Rocha leans at an angle against the wall and follows the slant of the sun, which is sinking. And Rocha, too, sinks in his smock at the wall. I read goodness and sternness in his face, wit and roguery, and the experience of many years of life. Rocha explains the workings of his old typewriter, whose keycaps are still enclosed in rings. It is surrounded by a mountain of papers in dark, partly tied folders. Then Rocha picks up a folder, with considered caution opens the knot, lays the black ties aside, and opens up the folder. A heap of typewritten sheets approaches me. The sheets are compactly typed as though the precious material had to be completely used. Rocha smiles at me and says he had to rewrite all his notes, he no longer liked them, and they no longer met his present requirements. His diary. *The Creation of the World*, as he called it.

The creation of the world: again. The diary that covered fifty years of life: again.

Rocha shows me how he manages it. He writes the new manuscript, then cuts out each line carefully with scissors, and pastes it over the old line.

Sometimes the old lines shimmer through, but he has nothing against that. The creation of the world. Again, line by line, typed on the same typewriter and carefully cut out with the scissors and pasted over the old creation of the world.

I wanted to know from Rocha whether such a diary were treacherous, whether the writing did not resemble a striptease.

Rocha answers, "Unlike an unconstrained girl, the writer shows not his hidden charms, rather the phantasms that press him, the ugliest part of himself, his feelings of guilt, and his resentments. While the girl is dressed at the beginning of her presentation and naked at the end, the process of writing is the reverse. The writer is naked at the start and at the conclusion is dressed."

The more slanted the afternoon light becomes, the more slanted Rocha becomes, leaning in his smock against the wall. He was born beyond the mountains, Trás-os-Montes, the son of a day laborer, in one of the most impoverished regions of the country. I guess him to be about eighty.

Unfortunately, he could not agree at all with the creation of the world. Not with the present version. Rocha tells why.

He tells about the village school, about his time as a servant on an estate, about grape picking, *Vindima*, and about a dream, traveling as a sailor over the planetary seas, meanwhile being stuck into a seminary for priests before he is sent to his uncle in Brazil, which becomes the Brazil of his torment. While Rocha leans ever more slanted, he remembers his years of apprenticeship and the time with his uncle in Santa Catarina beyond the great water. Armed with a revolver, the adolescent has to go through the nocturnal primeval forest into the city, slandered and opposed by his aunt, who practices black magic. During the evening ride to the post station, the growing lad dreams of Mary, the wife of the apothecary, who deceives her husband with the railway station manager. At night Rocha, in his chamber, writes love letters for the black house servants. The light becomes more and more slanted. At the age of eighteen Rocha returns, finishes his school diploma, and begins his study of medicine, makes contact with writers and with revolutionary ideas, helps found a newspaper, returns after the conclusion of his study to his village, where he is taken for a heretic, falls victim to village intrigues, can therefore not practice his profession, moves away again, has his first poems printed at his own expense, is forced into a rather long interruption by tuberculosis, enters a clinic, travels during his recovery through Spain, Italy, and France, before he returns to Salazar's Portugal, where he is soon arrested by the state police and imprisoned in Lisbon. In jail he imagines a raven: "He had chosen freedom, and since that moment had taken all the consequences of his choice upon himself. Sensible life was inextricably tied with the act of rebellion." That's what *The Creation of the World* was about, and something more that is not in history books. The afternoon is coming to an end. In his smock Rocha can scarcely keep his slanted position on the wall of the room. His countenance darkens. At the end, Rocha reads me something out of his folder in the late afternoon light. He doesn't read it, he sings it. In an extremely slanted position, in his smock at the wall, until it is almost dark in the room. Never have I heard a man read more marvelously. I admired that old man, and I trusted him, the Medico Especialista, Ouvidos, Nariz e Garganta, right behind the Ponte de Santa Clara in Coimbra.

And as far as rat poison is concerned, there is no tower from which I would not yet have leaped, no express train before which I would not yet have thrown myself, no corner of a platform that would not have enticed me magically. I already saw myself lying on the rails, and my spine was twisted in a grotesque way as though a great force had tried to turn it in a spiral. But to the potato peelers of Macao the idea of a natural death is completely alien. I know, I'm getting carried away. Only a suicide can assert that in a literal sense. The decisive step is perpetration. But such a *salto mortale* always wants an audience, wants a gallery: Step right up, ladies and gentlemen, come in and see, and be amazed. A Lusitanist is swallowing rat poison. Ridiculous as the knight of the mournful shape. Fanfare of trumpets and roll of drum. If you love this man, ladies and gentlemen, you must follow him in death right now. Otherwise you won't take him seriously, even as a corpse. The flirtatious tracts about suicide that situate the suicide even outside of grammar are of no use. How easily do they contain something of blackmail. To me, melancholia, as the slow, wasting death with open eyes, is a worse death. Who has the guts to break with the world? A suicide is always out of place and at the end even tortures himself with the question of style: poison or rope? The clean-sweep mood plays that kind of trick and makes suicide a mind game for those left behind. Whether it is a suicide disguised as an accident or a deed in plain view: When the absurdity once becomes certainty, it can become passion. No one likes to take leave, no one willingly parts from friends—if there are any at all—from the beloved, from one's own life. Nevertheless, I cannot rid myself of the suspicion that every suicide, at the end, glances again at the reaction of the living. I myself am the best proof of that. I lived more easily with the grace of never being my own observer. And what possibilities remain for those left behind? Either the dead man is damned or the living profit by death and are glad of it; hardly anyone tries to dissuade you; no one has any understanding of your deed. Someone standing poised to leap looks with binoculars turned around at the world, which has shrunken to the size of a toy. But is it not the gigantic toy that the would-be suicide cannot abide, because it has become too burdensome for him?

In his seminar he had tried to read stories of suicide with his students. It was a total failure. He remembers the dull faces of the young people in his lectures, in which I seemed more and more ridiculous to myself, like a gymnastics demonstrator who had to perform his dislocations for the entertainment of spoiled brats; like an oafish clown who had to let his ears be boxed equally by the director and the audience, to the general joy of all; like a yoked ass that must keep going in a circle from sunup to sundown. He remembers the childlike enthusiasm with which he had talked about books. After a few years of instruction he had arrived at the firm conclusion that more than half of all students should be expelled immediately, because they are just stupid. But what was he to do: The superiors in his secondary school never grew tired of recruiting more and more new students with all kinds of crude tricks to get chummy with them, even going on a drinking spree with them, sounding them out about colleagues, screwing one or another female student through an examination.

He had come upon traces of stupidity everywhere, until he decided to research them. He had been able to observe the worst possible effect of stupidity among his highly educated colleagues: when they mated with power for the sake of the cheap bitterness of reputation. The dumb ones always won. So stupidity had appeared to him soon as something primeval, and the palace of stupidity seemed to him no less expansive than the halls of state. He believed he could watch stupidity growing daily. Nobody escaped it; it had its fingers in the pie everywhere. If you thought you had cut off one of its heads, then seven grew in its place. He knew that stupidity existed. He had met it. And its sister was named vanity. Hope no longer seemed to be the driving force of history and progress to him, rather stupidity. With seven-league boots it strode ahead throughout the world, never squabbled with contradictions, but embraced them. Stupidity is indivisible; it is a cause, not an effect. It is the sickness of the strong and wants always to be only itself. For each and everyone it has its place. The university proved it. It gulps up everything and returns nothing. But above all, it murdered sense, for the dummy is a slicer of sense. Disturbingly the realization remained of having to spend his life under the tyranny of stupidity without any kind of hope.

How did I come to my mistaken course of study? How could I fall victim to Lusitanics? Somewhere in his paternal library, when he was a pupil, he had come upon sentences he later asserted set the switches on the rail of his life, sentences that he could not turn loose, sentences that intoxicated him and made him greedy with enthusiastic longing, sentences that drifted around him aimlessly, like his peers around the short skirts of the girls: O, *Lisbon, thou happy city, how beautiful art thou still. Dying thou sittest on the throne that was set up for thee by nature and history, but thy expired smile is still full of majesty.*

No, it was something else that had made him into a Lusitanist: It was the great earthquake, whose foreshocks he still felt in his own bones. Lisbon, founded by Odysseus as the capital city of the shipwrecked, for shipwreck is the only chance in the life of a man. The image of the weariness of bygone peoples had attracted him, the earthquake ground that calls might and reputation into question at every turn, longing for downfall; the demon behind the half-opened window shutters. Misfortune creates space here. He wanted to study it, and he suspected dimly that he would know his way about there one day. The expired smile, the beauty of being unhappy, the world called into question. That was his specialty.

Only later came the all-decisive reading of *Don Quixote*, from which everything came and into which everything was to flow.

He no longer wanted to live alone in the wind that fell gray over the mountains and into the country; I no longer wanted just to wait for my life. Love ceases eternally. He said that to himself, as though he had two tongues in his mouth, and he hung with his hotel room high in the darkness. What kind of paths were those he traveled in his daily routine? Taxi trips over cat-head-sized paving stones to and from the university, paths of my blindly enraged absentmindedness during lectures and seminars, paths through the swamp of a provincial soggy mass that called itself the University of Thulsern, where the doctoral orals were finished diagonally on the beds, where there was envious observation of just who was with whom and against whom. A dissertation was being debated, stimulated by a professor who no longer wanted to endorse it because he had another female candidate at work who wouldn't leave him alone, nor he her. But the doctoral candidate was a bosom friend of the professor's past student, whose son, a years-long assistant to the professor, wanted to pass the examination, and all of that widely gossiped in the anterooms, a long exchange of letters back and forth, attacks, rectifications, denunciations, all the way up to the rector, farther on to the ministry, on to the UNO, and then the feminist adherents who were not ashamed to let themselves be mounted by the mightiest bulls, if it just produced something, a seat on a panel here, a special vote there. All that made him weary and sulky. He felt his weariness as a weight in his bones; he paused, and sat as still as a bird in its nest. Again and again his weariness bent over him; it was his steady companion. He was also tired of his vocation. Thoughts did not stand on their own legs there but used the crutches of secondary literature: "I base my remarks on..." Such thoughts were descendants of traditional ways of thinking, accepted in an exemplary way, sacrosanct, blessed by a council that had not only empowered itself for that purpose but likewise crept along on crutches, thought on crutches, and lashed out with those crutches as well. The discipline had become a game of mean old men on crutches. But even he submitted and made a pretty curtsy. His colleagues on the faculty appeared to him like the grotesque masks of a spook train. In their presence, in general, he thought he was constantly at a carnival, being thrust into a senseless commotion in which anything was permitted, because all the bounds of shame had long ago fallen. That was the worst thing about university life: He knew it, he knew each and every one, there were no more surprises, nothing new, nothing that had excited the mind or made the heart beat faster, beat a hundred times, everything was said, done, discussed, known, lived, deceased, dead. He knew that life so well he could vomit. When in recent times he had entered the departmental building, his loathing had risen in him and had stuck like a frog in his throat. There it sat and could move neither forward nor back. The university was a chain-swing carrousel on which the same ones always revolved around the same thing. The copier boys knew long ago about the provincial jokes and bed stories, acted pretentiously with them, swaggered, and were nosy. All the professors carry on a steady scolding and shrieking. And quiet and modesty are a requirement for a philological existence. But the ladies and gentlemen whom he knew saw in literary works only a substitute life. What for them was the subject of a lecture or an essay was for him life itself. But the others believed they recognized a world of significance in literature without being affected by it in that they see the happiness of the interpreter. But it is only the megalomania of the interpreter. Philologists believe they can not only serve a thing but can exert power with it as well. As soon as they hold a high position and can call themselves professors, they know nothing more than their classic entrance into a bondaged auditorium, they peer at the admiring gazes, especially those of the world of ladies in the front rows, and use the lecture hall solely to compensate for their asceticism and to satisfy their vanity. Their favorite place is neither the research cell nor the library, rather the racetrack of vanity, the fencing and gymnastic court of lust for power, the transshipping port for smuggled scandal and gossip goods, the takeoff and landing strip of their academic aerobatics: the photocopier. Where once one gathered around the village linden tree, now one meets at this Ark of the Covenant of scholarly method. Whenever there is a paper jam, research ceases at once. Then they stand there, scientific bureaucrats and faculty sulks. The lemurs in the brick rotundas, in the provisionally tileless maternity wards, in the scientific bunkers that rear heavenward with carefully hidden entrances like parking towers, then hastily demand epaulettes, whisper and preen for a while before they fade out. Their arrogance is comparable to the beetle that, when the sultan's stallion was about to be shoed, saw his opportunity coming and stuck out his little foot. And again and again they profess a rite of initiation: nerves instead of foreskin. With that they chastise their successors and create them in the jelly glasses of their discipline after their own image and semblance: the sycophant and complier, the informer and auditor of glory, flawed speaker and earwitness, the paper drunk and secret poet who keeps his precious poems as though they were his first condom. A smart man once compared professors to sled dogs that hardly pulled a couple of times before raising a leg for every imaginable kind of business, so that you couldn't move from the spot at all with the beasts.

Once upon a time the Lord God had a wonderful idea: He created a being that could live only by his whims and was decently paid for that. He created the professor. But then the Devil came and said he had a much better idea. And he created the colleague.

That world finally lay behind him. It was a farewell without regret.

I left: a ridiculous figure.

His university, the professors: nothing but state corpses.

When he thought of them, he had to laugh. A few days a week he pretended to his colleagues and his students to be a man who did not really exist in actuality at all. He existed only in their imagination. The role was called: Professor of Lusitanics. He played the role, which he sketched week after week, month after month, year after year at the moment when there was a dress rehearsal. But there never was even a dress rehearsal, for the dress rehearsal was always simultaneously the premiere. He played the role as hero in a series. And he wore himself out like a hero in a series.

And today you see, ladies and gentlemen, the professor at the point of despair. Shhhh! He just pretended to be something to all of them that he himself wasn't at all, rather that he just made up only for them and for himself. And every one of them fell for it after his appointment. Nobody could take that triumph away from him. He played the role well. Very slowly he had grown into it and in the end was playing it so well that he himself fell for it. It was the role of his life.

But every man dies his own death. For him it began so simply and routinely that for a while he took the end for the beginning of a new season. But the game was over. Had taken wing.

Curtain.

I left, as though he were waiting until age scratched his face apart and everything flew away from him. He had become restless because of the emptiness in him and around him; sluggishly he sat on park benches and in hotel lobbies, in cafés and bars, turned on bath water aimlessly, lay in the tub until he got cold, and he looked at clocks, again and again at clocks, observed their regular ticking, stared at the pendulum and the second hand until he got dizzy, and from that he gathered that he was still alive. I'm fine, he wrote on postcards home that he never mailed; he strolled through strange cities, pedestrian zones, let the gutter flow past him, tramped through elegant shops and passages, breathed the vapor of buildings, sat forlorn on the edges of hotel beds, and watched as darkness fell slowly over the rooftops and thrust him even deeper; he strode through corridors, sometimes tried the handles of locked doors, wandered around aimlessly on the afternoons after his lecture, returned late to his boardinghouse, in which only traveling salesmen spent the night, with whom he had no contact, not even at the morosely eaten breakfast in a conservatory; there he hid behind a newspaper, even read the business section if necessary, of which he understood not a word, just not to have to look up, tremblingly poured coffee into his cup or choked on a bread roll, sneaked up to his room again long after supper, left the light in the bathroom burning all night long so he wouldn't be all by himself, locked the door, turned the key twice and fastened the security chain, heard music that penetrated through walls, sometimes the groaning of a pair of lovers, was lured into back streets, stopped enthralled, had intoxicating symphonies in his ear, saw wonderfully glowing pictures within reach in front of his eyes, watched the gait of fascinating women—but nothing was true—saw girls who smiled at him and embedded him in their wild hair, all the while meaning someone else, had the foot-worn sidewalks to himself, ran back and forth through a cold city, always new paths, until he paused breathlessly and noticed that he had gotten hopelessly lost and thoroughly disoriented while he was watching how dead lights intermingled and advertising texts shouted ownme, buyme, takeme, looked for regularities in his half-lived days, recognized that everything had become indistinguishable in weeks, months, years. I have wasted my life, he could be heard to say, had anyone been listening to him, and his whole half-lived life seemed to him to consist of nothing but little habits. To have great affection for something means to invite misfortune, as when one watches a snail, he thought coldly; its feelers are stretched out and it sails on a silken, slimy path, and in the next moment back into its house, no more sentences that burned on the tongue like forbidden kisses, no more incredible presumptions, and the alcohol whispered words to him that he had not known previously; it mixed the colors and could stretch walls like rubber, and besides helped him reach a painfully clear consciousness of himself in momentary flashes, a twofold numbness and a long silence, thus an interior speaking that seemed final. He sneaked over cemeteries, read names and dates, and *Man proposes, God disposes* was on his parents grave at home in the Thulsern Cemetery, in which he wanted to be buried for not much money. He pointed to graves that he didn't know, and there was no one who could have watched him doing it or could have followed his hint, no arm opened for him, *they are all gone*; and often he tried to imagine life in strange houses, but immediately saw nothing but the base acts of ordinariness; and when he crouched on the edge of a curb, it seemed that his thoughts caught on one word or another or on a gesture for which he hungered. More and more frequently he sat in bars, left too much money there, requested songs from glittering faraway singers, went through his list of song requests. They were nothing at all but trivial pop tunes for which he still had a weak sentiment, *and so I face the final curtain*. He became smaller and smaller, shriveled before the eyes of blind pianists, turned cold and lonely, *I did it my way*, believed for a few seconds that he had the sun at his back and a bold wind all about him, *send in the clowns*. Does one really need people to make a world, he implored a barmaid in her makeup, and again and again he wanted to smoke up his time and drown himself in the glass in front of him. Someone was involved in a long, intoxicated story, the end of which he would have liked to hear, but he was on top, he told himself, had at a young age become a professor, received prizes from academies, been invited to international conferences—why, he had everything, he had even more, much more, than he needed, he had the peak, which would become an abyss to him, filled with his emptiness, where the worms of discontent waited, blackness behind the eyes. And the drunken man finally found the resolution of his story, began to hum, finally to sing, and in the end to bawl out: *The ship that always sets its sails stiffly on my cap, that ship's called dying. I drink to drive the evil dream out of the nighttime pain. The world is but a pale stream. The sun is dying, nothing will remain.*

Suddenly a man with European features is approaching him, reminiscent of my college friend Herzig: an encounter after years in which contact had been broken. And Herzig told about his visit to Siena. Years before he had once been in Siena, Herzig says breathlessly. Herzig was always breathless: born on Lake Constance, student of art history, Romance languages, philosophy in Tübingen, Paris, and Munich, lecturer in Aix-en-Provence, Toulouse, Milan, and Nice, dragon researcher on the Upper Rhine. When he thought back on Siena, Herzig says, he saw the overly slender tower at the Piazza del Campo, where it was leaning to the side before the hastily retreating strands of a thunderstorm. Before the campanile threatened to plunge into an unexpected, impending crackle, he, Herzig, had fled into a side street: to his Madonnas. Three hundred meters, Palazzo Buonsignori, the art gallery. Thirty-seven halls, and in every hall at least three or four times a *Madonna col bambino*. But it wasn't because of those Mothers of God, rather because of the bird squashing. You see, Mary—there were, by the way, exclusively rustic, if not to say ugly, Marys among them. The painters had presumably taken their models from the surrounding villages—Mary always had the Baby Jesus in her arms, and the Baby Jesus had a songbird in his hand, says Herzig. Well, the bird *in* his hand or *on* his hand. At first the bird sat, according to Herzig, pertly on an outstretched finger, but the Mother of God carried her Son light as a feather, even regally. But then, from picture to picture, a sickness spread that must until now have escaped the eyes of all experts, for he, Herzig, in spite of enthusiastic effort, had been able to find no scholarly literature about it. The copied likenesses of the peasant girls became from picture to picture coarser, uglier, more scarred, and less respectable. Besides, they seemed to forget how one held a child in one's arms. The Baby Jesus, too, became from picture to picture broader browed, more apathetic, more brutal, and more monstrous. From picture to picture he, Herzig, could observe how the Baby Jesuses, who finally developed into fat infants with the spitefully petrified faces of old men, more and more closed their repulsive patty-cake hands about the bird, how those repugnant sausage fingers from picture to picture throttled the bird's throat more and more. And Herzig had wondered, at the sight of the series *Madonna col bambino*, why the development had not proceeded in the opposite way: One painter could certainly have learned from the other. Now, without having contacted me for years, Herzig is reflecting about whether he ought not to devote an essay to the bird squashing, since the phenomenon had escaped the world of specialists until now, as little as he could understand that. Meanwhile, he was still looking for the blue of an egg.

The train traveled from Lisbon to Macao, and I feuded with God as in a medieval mystery play. Again one of my books happens into my hands. At the end the professor had read from it to the students in his seminar, and already he opened up the book wrapped in packing paper and read it like a breviary:

"Lord, life is hurting me. I am sitting in this compartment, *single special*, in a box, naked and alone in the night, a blind man who is being carried to a blind city, to Macao. Naked and alone in the night I lie with crossed arms on a mattress and wait, I, for whom no one anywhere is waiting, I am waiting for Thee in the darkness, Thou, Whose existence I have always stubbornly denied and in Whom I even now do not believe, Thou Invisible One, Who hast withdrawn from Thy creation. I see Thee in every beam of the light of a brief train stop, in every lamp in a tunnel, I see Thee red and green in signals and rail switches, I pray to Thee in the litany of the wheels. Lord, what words do I line up without measure or goal just to manage a bit of company for myself, to be less alone in my soliloquy with Thee. So here I am, plunged deeply into the tar-black of my last night. Lord, for how many years have we been waging this duel, without seeing one another...like a dog fighting with the shadow of his tail, Lord, and lifting unequal weapons against one another: Thee, Thy privilege of not being, I its opposite, namely of being. Alone. The quarrel of a deaf man with a mute. Lord, I am on my deathbed, and I have hesitated far too long for this, because nobody could tell me about the grass, and because I went along with the subterfuge, although everything is after all in vain. Lord, if I succeeded just once in playing the fool, sitting at Thy feet, with bells and in a costume of patches—but the rope becomes shorter and shorter, the eye of the needle narrower, Lord—with a red and a black shoe."

A warm wind came up.

The sky was blanketed.

I believed I had never had such a wind on my face.

A dog rambled around me, looked at me with cunning eyes before he slunk away.

The professor felt an almond-bitter taste on his tongue.

Great distances always lured me: the farther away from this Thulsern, the better.

I enjoyed Australia with its corrupt blue sky. Canada overpowered me with its desolate expanses. I loved New Zealand because it is so young. I would like to have had a house on the Bay of Islands with a blue roof, whitewashed walls, and a veranda from which I could look directly at the gentle bay.

The boat to Hong Kong is getting underway.

I have no return-trip ticket.

Macao is now as though drawn with a pencil.

I never saw such a decrepit city.

Not even Surabaya can keep up with Macao.

How often have I run around this tongue of land.

I would like to die on the spot.

A young woman walks past, almost a girl still, with a supple gait, slender, straight legs and a noticeably good figure. Only, her face is full of pimples. What does one fall in love with, when one falls in love, Mary?

There is a smell of tar and rags.

He has reached the warehouses.

His first attempts with ice skates.

How he always kept buckling to the side.

And my brother can skate faultlessly backward.

The ice is very rough.

With effort move ahead, reach with my left leg, slide off with my right.

I can't do anything right, and my brother laughs.

I would like to have had a hockey stick to prop myself up with.

Most of all I would like to be the puck.

Slapped by the stick of the player, I slithered smoothly over the ice until another stick stopped me, shoved me back and forth, craftily flipped me through the legs of an opponent before he could give me a mighty swat that would make me rebound from the web until the referee would take me in his hand, stroke me a bit, and finally throw me again between the sticks. While a puck struck me and slit my lower lip, while a bit of blood dripped onto the ice and left behind little dark red spots along which one could have skated on ice skates, while I had to be carried from the ice, while my lip was sewed up, while my father was even somewhat proud of me, while he told me that it soon would no longer hurt, for soon grass would cover it all, my brother was thinking about how the ice rink could be roofed over with a bridge of glass.

The Hotel Bela Vista is the Grand Hotel Thanatos and sends off business letters:

"Dear Sir, if we turn to you today, it is not by chance, rather because we have received information about you that permits us to hope that our services can be useful to you. You will surely have experienced that in human existence circumstances can arise that seem to even the most courageous man so desperate that any struggle against them seems futile and the thought of death a liberation. Close your eyes, sleep, never wake up, no more questions, no reproaches.... Many people, just between us, cherished this dream and wished it ardently to come true.... However, with the exception of very few cases, people do not dare liberate themselves from their suffering, and that's understandable, if you observe those who have tried it. For most attempts at suicide fail in a gruesome way. Suicide is an art that is a mystery to the average man, that from its nature, too, forbids collecting experiences with it. We, dear sir, are prepared to furnish you with those experiences, in case, as we believe, you are interested in this problem. As owners of a hotel in Macao that, because of the particular circumstances of its geographical and political situation, is removed from any distressing inspection, we have considered that it is our duty to put at the disposal of people who for serious and incontrovertible reasons are intent on giving up their lives the means that allow them without pain and, we might almost say, without risk to carry out their plan. In our hotel, death while sleeping awaits you under the most pleasant conditions. It is sufficient upon your arrival to deposit $500. That sum relieves you of all expenses during your stay with us, the length of which remains unknown to you. In closing, permit us to mention further that our hotel lies in a landscape of choice beauty. Please announce your arrival three days in advance."

Here I am, dear manager.

And the potato-peeling Chinese woman doubtless belongs to the discreet personnel.

I will not return to Thulsern.

It is dark. In the deep quiet I hear nothing but the pounding of my heart.

All the objects stay silent to me.

The bed is silent and the chest, the desk, the suitcase, the curtains are silent: in defiance of me, to scorn me.

Slowly death begins to circle me.

Cautiously he gropes toward me, soft and unnoticeable.

He is a master of quiet deception.

At times I look up to see whether he is spying on me.

I peer into the darkness.

I look for the silhouette of a shadow there.

Soon he will come.

What will they find in this room?

A corpse, pale and cold.

The ridiculous thing I was once has arrived at its destination.

That decisive hour will hold no terror; calm down, Professor.

Inside you will become gray and dubious, and behind the mask of gentle irony and courtesy the last threads of life and happiness will break.

On into the darkness.

Without waiting for words of comfort.

Only defeats are reliable.

What would not become tranquil, whenever one distanced oneself?

Then he felt a nausea rising in him, as though any moment he would vomit his insides.

Suddenly his body glowed with fever; flatulence broke out of him and tainted the air, enshrouded him in a cloud of sulfur and decay.

While he tried to sweat out his fever, the salvos of the laughter of his listeners in the lectures came to his mind again, when in a dreary lecture hall he imparted his thoughts on *Don Quixote*.

With cramped bowels he let the ridicule pass over him, tried to speak against it with a voice cracked with fever, but he failed miserably.

He talked to himself.

When had he left the hotel again?

Why was he leaning on the wall of this building?

Why was he roaming through this Macao?

He wanted to go back.

He was weary and wanted to lie down.

Just sleep.

But he had gotten lost.

It cost him some effort to make his way back to his hotel with questions.

A rare serenity lay in the air.

It is difficult for him to move from the spot.

He is afraid of collapsing any moment.

But then he emerges again into the aromatic symphony of a rotting Macao.

Innumerable odors of decay mixed into a single stench of ruin.

Vapors came from the sewers, the smell of boiling gelatin, burned rubber, and smoldering rags mixed with that of a slaughterhouse; in addition there come rotting garbage, the moldering cadaver of a cat, over-ripe fruit.

He begins to understand.

He had to travel to Macao in order to understand Europe in the last shabby corner of Europe, to which he belonged, which had spit him out.

Now he was at the place to experience ruin

directly, to see it, smell it, touch it.

Macao as a symbol of Europe.

This frivolous beehive of empty busyness: at the end.

Fallen to a gambling den.

Misery camouflaged with growth and progress, ravaged, defiled like the flayed face of enlightenment that has been covered with the scab of technocracy. Europe stood for naught but blindness and arrogance, and whatever interfered was swept under the luxurious rug of prosperity. Sulkiness had learned to be corrupted and sold as contentment. Europe was like his ridiculous university: There were no more riddles and no purposes. Everything was so falsely arranged and interwoven with supposed rules.

He heard music, but the music sounded spurious.

It did not move him, although the voices sounded lovely and mixed with the wind in the trees.

He would have liked to wave a baton, but the music sounded spurious.

He looked for the right sound, he looked for harmony behind the distortion, but he did not find them.

It sounded spurious as the laurel was spurious that grew from great tubs and made him think of a crematorium, of a hall of the last benediction, where the dead were ushered out with clever sermons.

The wind blew a dirty newspaper across the street; two dirty politicians shook hands on the dirty front page.

A policeman was standing bored in a smart uniform on a corner, and he revealed the stupid and arrogant face of all policemen.

On the strand the corpse of the young girl had perhaps washed up. And her spine was twisted in a grotesque way, as though someone had tried to turn it into a spiral.

A heavy, black limousine turned into the street: soundless, a dully gleaming coffin with drawn curtains, highly polished.

Is that how casino millions are moved?

Was the car part of a money laundering?

The automobile was in no way different from the coach of an ambassador; perhaps a diplomat was even sitting on the back seat, a financial magnate, a briber or someone bribed, or was it the Sultan of Brunei, the richest land on earth.

The car stopped.

Bodyguards surveyed the street, one opened the door, at the ready, a soldier.

In a dark suit, finest cloth, made by the best tailor, a slight little man was being protected. A miserable nothing who must have been afraid for his paltry life, protected from—

maybe the professor, who is standing on the street and has swallowed rat poison.

A stray dog wanders around the limousine, a

cloud moves in front of the sun, a vaporous veil dissolves the scene.

What he heard were dissonances, impure noises that quarreled with one another, a tenacious experiment for which he had no understanding.

Everything was fragile from the beginning and wasted in a ridiculous manner.

A beggar opened his dirty hollow hand.

The professor handed him a disproportionate sum, thought of indulgence, and felt the bad conscience of the rich European, and he was ashamed not to have given more.

He longed to dine elegantly.

His voracious orgies came like seizures.

He would have liked to sit in the sun, on the terrace of an expensive, the most expensive, restaurant, as he had once enjoyed sitting on the Piazza Navona, admiring the oval of the arena and drinking his *Corvo Duca di Salaparuta* with thoughts on the slain gladiators. Afterward, the *professore*, completely surrounded by heroic antiquity, had walked down shadowy lanes, past butcher shops in which slit-open carcasses were hanging, fresh and cool sacrificial animals. In the hotel he had lain down on the bed and relished his weariness, the heaviness of his limbs, the light that had fallen through the blinds of half-closed window shutters. He remembered having fallen into a long slumber and there having dreamed of his death that—he was quite certain—would overtake him in one hotel or another.

He longed for soft carpets and fabric-covered walls, like the damask of a bed in a first-class hotel.

His eyes teared up, dwindling gray.

You could have throttled the girls of Macao at their waists, they were so slender.

He imagined their stone-hard breasts; he thought of the dark nipples, just the size of a coin; and he thought of alluring undergarments that seemed to be made for dolls.

He was sweating all over, on his face and into his shoes, on his thighs, under his arms, between his legs.

He was afraid of the odor of his body.

Was that already the odor of death, or was this merely the stink of a goat?

What he saw were almond eyes.

Step right up, open up your mouth, just stop soon.

The rules of life of his father, who had neglected to tell him about the grass.

A flagpole rose against a hazy sky.

In his ridiculous getup the professor looked like a candidate for confirmation.

Even more ridiculous than the untouched classics bound in leather in his father's glass bookcase.

After his confirmation they had dressed him in this ridiculous way. Even the dead laughed at him.

By watching, he learned about the attitudes of men. In the streets only the wind spoke. The ocean led directly into the sky, and he stood there, wanted to run on from here, on and on. On the wall of a building a picture of Jesus was hanging, which threatened to fall any moment. Next to it a damp spot, like a map.

His gaze fell upon the revolving door of a casino.

The white gloves of the doorman gleamed.

The operetta uniform gleamed. Braid and shoulder straps, aiguillette and cummerbund. Swing open, swing closed, always in a circle, *have fun, enjoy your stay.* A dark, opaque tipping power emanated from the doorman. Gentlemen clad in black left the casino. Pistol carriers.

In front of the bar stood fragile, colorful chairs. A girl sent her smile down the narrow street, her hair black as lacquer.

A lovely whore with a cold doll's face and a decently made-up mouth. Should he buy that Mary-mouth? He was too tired. He was a lout who could not even speak to a whore.

But he would have been ready to pay any price.

The girl disappeared into the bar; he continued.

The smile of the woman before his eyes.

He would not come back, he would not even turn around. One more missed opportunity. He walked along a dirty wall behind which he imagined a well-tended, shadowy garden that might belong to a rich Chinese, to one whom the colorful gambling chips and the desperation of losers had made fat. A gust of wind whirled dust up. The wall was covered. The professor was thirsty. His tongue was dry. He could have had a drink in the bar. Should he turn around, or would he just make himself ridiculous before the lovely whore, Mary. She would smile at him and know that he had not returned for the sake of his thirst. With a firm stride he arrived at the square in front of the church. His finger stroked crumbling walls. He went up the steps. He had once walked down the Spanish Steps. Rome had lain at his feet, the Eternal City, that tossing balloon. A child offered him a handful of puffed rice. Disgusted him. The puffed rice fell to the steps and, before the child could grab them, he had stepped on them. People crowded toward him. He bumped and was bumped. Where did they come from so suddenly? The smile of the lovely whore. It pursued him still; it had fastened onto the nape of his neck, in his memory; no, it didn't pursue him, it came toward him. Should he, because of a whore in Macao, again rise from among the dead? He suppressed his predatory cravings, hidden under the mask of the European philistine, of the ridiculous scholar. He was afraid that the lovely whore could see through him at the first attempt. She was lovely. Supple and slender. Doubtless she had hard tits, and a tar-black furry animal lurked between her immaculate thighs. A short-order cook was displaying wares. The professor believed that he recognized baked rain worms. They would immediately penetrate his body. He had to have a beer right now; only a beer would help him wash the worms down his throat into his stomach, into his intestines. The lovely whore forced the professor onto his knees, and she dictated to him what he willingly, obediently, and hopelessly fallen put onto paper as his testament. For the fraction of a second the short-order cook was the person whom he would like to have been. He remembered the large, cold kitchen in his parents' house, the floor of which always stank of ammonia. Unintentionally he imagined how grass broke through the kitchen tiles, how the grass began to overrun the kitchen; he let it grow higher and higher in his imagination. Already he was walking barefoot through the morning dew, and on the walls dandelions and primroses were blooming. The door opened, and his mother entered in a wheelchair, almost soundlessly, but got stuck in the high grass, and instead of yelling she began with a soft voice to hum her favorite song until finally she carefully formed the words: Not everyday is Sunday, not everyday is there wine. But everyday you must love me and be just mine. Then she called out the name of my brother. The professor admonished himself to be correct, but his thoughts did not obey, rather went their way in Macao's stricken greatness, went over the river and the hills, over the Chinese frontier, went farther and farther, went halfway around the world to Thulsern, where death began to throw his net over the professor, past the people in building entrances, past the clusters of people in the gambling dens. The net flew past, pressing and shoving and rubbing, past shrill laughter of embarrassment on the part of the Asiatics; obscene words slipped through the mesh, questions and answers trundled down the street, dreams soared like pigeons and disappeared behind the counter of a cheap bar between the thighs of a long-legged, narrow-hipped, spraddle-legged lovely whore surrounded by luckily dumb pimps and wooers wearing undershirts, who dignifies them, however, with no glance, rather has her eye on the European conqueror's instinct, on the missionary position, by letting her smile smile down the narrow street. Macao was ready to be conquered by this smile, to surrender to it, to sell itself to it.

I thought of coarseness, of anxiety, greed, and crime. What if someone struck him down and robbed him at this moment. He would not resist, rather would resign himself to the blows and kicks and stabs, and hope to fall unconscious very quickly. Perhaps his murderer was already on the way, perhaps he was lurking for him already; perhaps his murderer was a petty thief who, at the moment when he would plunge his dagger into his abdomen, balanced the books of all his depressions. The net flew past the shadows, the obstacles and the underbrush, also past the harassed murderer, who soon would crumple under the batons of the police. The professor fled from the sight of people; he fled the eye of his invisible murderer, the windows and doors that are nothing more than lusting eyes, the trash on the street, the smeared walls, the gutter, the trees, the stench from the river, the honking and noise. You're alive, alive, he said to himself with disbelief. Ponderously he moved through the smells of oil and dough and fast food; thick white beans glared at him, slippery in oil, floating in a brew of vinegar, smelled fishy; stinking of grease the noodles curled around mouths like adders, soft and sloppy and fatty, were devoured by lips like the tongues of lovers. Perhaps he should go to the nearest telephone and call. Call anybody, hear a human voice, a trusted European voice; he would press the buttons of the telephone or turn the dial; that sound alone would bring safety, the clicking in his ear, the hum of the line, then the ringing. But what if nobody picked up on the other end; what if none of the somebodies were at home; what if the line were busy for hours, the line failed, just went dead? He again felt on top of things because he did not telephone; he had conquered his thoughts; all nonsense, he had said, no one is being murdered here, here I'm safe; I've condemned myself; I've swallowed rat poison; the pharmacist is my friend, my ally, my savior. So he wandered on, wandered into an engulfed street gut, filled with stinking cars, trucks, people, many too many people, people like maggots, people whom this gut digested in the maelstrom of the traffic; he was jostled but did not turn around, accepted it indifferently, seemed to be the only one going in the wrong direction; all the others were approaching him; he saw headlights turned on in broad daylight, heard transmissions clacking; gears were shifted; he heard the din of hoarse honking, breathed the frenzy, the impatience, had lost direction and time, was beamed on, was abused by drivers, cursed, but pushed on, looking for the angel of prophecy, the guardian angel, but did not find him. No angel of the Lord appeared and no sign in the heavens, and the earth had not opened up. Dirty walls accompany me. He wanted to pray, but God was not there, was denied by the smile of the lovely whore. *Starfish I greet you, oh Mary, help*. But his Mary was made of wood and plaster, and the worms had already drilled her labyrinth. Motor scooters clattered past. Again he hurried up and down steps, saw sumptuous cakes in the displays, thought about kindergarten birthdays, about blowing out candles, and his plea: Father, tell me about the grass. There was an odor of latrines. In front of a monument he felt the grandeur of history, believed suddenly in its icy breath;

buildings that seemed built for eternity stared at him and laughed at him in his misery. People lived for their businesses, lived for their pleasures; what did he have in common with them? Behind rolled-down shutters life went on without stopping; it could not be stopped, not done away with. Life, everywhere, even in the dirt, there above all. Someone was peeling a tuber; there was a smell of leek, of onion breath, and of garlic belches; and while that person was peeling, he was forming long, complicated sentences that applied to someone or other; the professor could not recognize to whom. The man ate up his tuber, dipped the stalk into a cup and handed the tip to the dog that lay at his feet. Gratification spread over the man's face; revolting gratification, I thought, and was shot through with envy. My steps echoed, his shadow ran before him; he chased after it, while the shadow snuck off to the side and finally was following him. From a fountain water dripped, typhoid water possibly; on the side of the fountain an old man was leaning, as though he were freezing under his slimmed-down headgear. The old man was standing in slippers and was blind; he could have been taken for a priest because of his dignity and his tattered cloak. I have an eye for priests. Since my childhood I can smell clerical garb. He did not like priests, kept them at a safe distance, as though they were contagious, avoided them, mistrusted them thoroughly, held them for false and sly, avaricious and lecherous. Their white hands repulsed him.

The water murmured transitoriness.

Where had he picked up that sentence? Dirty flies were humming; in the buildings rats were probably mating; the water resembled vomited beer foam. With a snappy motion of his hand a youth drew a snake in the air, then he pulled a bundle of bills from his pocket, hastily counted the tattered money, handed it to someone else, took something in return, grinned, showing gold teeth. My hands rushed at my face. My hair was wet with sweat, clung and pricked my forehead; the lenses of my glasses were misted over. Children in blue school uniforms and white knee socks streamed past. Cute to look at, tiny, but threatening as a pack. Once, in Rome, Porta Portese, he had had to defend himself against a horde of trained child thieves who had already encircled him. He could not strike out, a bigger brother would have been on the spot immediately. So only one thing was left for him: To take off. Children with smooth faces, next to them an old woman with ravaged skin, emaciated, with the head of a monkey skull, a ghost. The teacher. Into her mouth she stuffed something that looked like the end of a sausage. And I felt hunger; I was in the mood for a bag of roasted almonds from the Christmas market, all the ways home seemed to lead past Christmas; damn the Feast of Peace. He longed for something sweet, for chocolates, marzipan bread, for expensive candy. The children seemed to him like toys; he doubted that they were of flesh and blood, so very much did they seem plastic imitations. And he behaved as though he had to disappear in Macao, as though he had a lot to answer for, as though he were a ravisher of children, a murderer of whores, or a spy. No, he had shoved his mother in her wheelchair into the abyss, tipped her over a bridge railing into the depths. He felt guilty. That's why I'm wandering through this city, taking wrong turns into dead-end streets, straying through backyards and remote corners. The shot that I took at my father because he didn't tell me about the grass was swallowed up by the noise of Macao. Nobody took note of my murder. I am infamous. And with that sky above. He ought to be locked up. If I were just finally sitting in my hotel. I would clap the wooden, weather-beaten Macao window shutters closed and shut out the world; and he remembered a German chorus that had sung *Am Brunnen vor dem Tore* in the middle of the night: Was it in front of the titans of the Fontana di Trevi or where—I no longer knew. Perhaps I also just read it. I never experienced my linden tree, I never arrived at the gates; I have experienced the world only in books. But they had thought of home with a tender heart while far away, thought of the well and the linden tree, and the German god had seemed near enough to touch. Flies danced about him like a sneer. In Macao there was no chorus. The fuckers of children had gotten out in Bangkok or flown on to Manila. Someone was strewing sawdust onto the street mire. At once human legs tromped down the sawdust, stomped around on it, carried it farther on their soles like a secret message; a broom swept over a narrow street, lightly wielded from the wrist of a woman like a foil. Presumably the smiling, lovely whore was now counting her money and looking down the narrow street with eyes that no one could resist. Her smile still tortures me. I still have not succeeded in escaping it. What may the room look like in which the lovely whore serves her clients; how may it be when she peels off her slit dress; what may it smell like in that temporary lodging; does it smell like male sweat and sperm, like cheap wine or inexpensive perfume? He would have liked to wash, at least his hands; they were sticky, as though he had been canning marmalade; he would have liked to cool his forehead with a damp cloth, would have liked to open his shirt and dry his chest, massage his heart, but he couldn't do it because the lovely whore would have been looking on, because a thousand Macao eyes were looking at him, and because there was no water there into which he could have dipped his hands up to his elbows; there was, you see, no water there because the kitchen was overgrown by grass, because it had become unusable despite all the tiles that always smelled like ammonia. But there was once a time when gods had inhabited that kitchen. He longed for the coolness of morning in the shadow of high buildings, for the colors and the wind of Lisbon, when the sun teases the roofs and brushes along the old walls. He would have liked to smell incense, the wax and the old robes in the sacristy, would have liked to see candles burning before dependable saints who always helped, if one just called them. He would have his shoes shined and go to the barber, buy a newspaper that still smelled like the printing plant, drink a coffee in a bar at a small polished marble table, take a seat next to perfumed men and nonchalantly watch the bustle. Later he would have a picnic lunch packed for him, bread, cold roast meat, some fowl, fruits, and wine, and drive out to Cascais or only to Belém, to watch the river flowing in the shadow of the tower and to have Vasco return with Camões on board.

But a mangy mongrel wag-tailed around him, a woman wearing a cornflower-blue dress brushed him lightly, European or American, but their eyes did not meet, however much he wished for it. He was sweating even more and, stopping briefly, wiped the sweat from his brow with the pocket handkerchief from his jacket. A bus vomited its passengers, who stood in bunches before slowly dispersing. Each one knew where to go; only he did not know. All around him busyness, dirty toes in dirty sandals, dirty hands, dirty clothes, dirty necks in dirty shirts, heat and dampness. Where could he have fled to? Brackish the water in the river, in which slain bodies floated with swollen bellies. An old woman was sitting on a stool, a youth with an apathetic face squatting beside her, as though he had in that instant had to relieve himself. His open mouth yawned to the sky; gnats swarmed around him; his eyes had an empty expression. The boy spat his spittle between his brown feet, remained unmoving in a squat, looked more imbecilic than a cab horse, gaped, grinned at me, showed his bad teeth. Dogs scuffled in the dirt. I noticed how a group of young men took notice of me surreptitiously from the corner of their eyes. All of them had mottled and scabby skin and awful teeth behind gaping lips. One quickly grabbed his genitals, enticing with an unmistakable gesture, grinned, let his hands circle his erection gently; his fingers were black with dirt. Everywhere those ravenous mouths. The lovely whore smiled at a black car that glided up like a panther, she smiled at the driver, who threw the door open, but skipped the smile and held his hat in front of his gray-uniformed chest. The lovely whore had disappeared.

Treason, croaked the birds over Macao.

Treasontreason.

And her smile was red as blood, white as snow, black as ebony. He would like to sit down at the river in a blossom-white suit of silk and watch the gloves of the traffic policemen, which flew back and forth like doves. Beauty queens sauntered, followed by diplomats, bankers, bankruptees, and he imagined setting fire to the large department store in front of the façade of which he had come to a stop. The arsonist was caught in the act, and the policeman with the white gloves led him off through a small street of gogglers. The professor knew that they would hit him and kick him and finally execute him; they would stand him at one of those grimy walls and shoot him down like a mangy dog. Not a single person would miss him. Music began again. Fashionably dressed people surrounded him. Had they come to his execution? Why were they encircling him? How had he gotten to this square, how to this church? But the church was not a church, rather a gambling casino, and the gentlemen wanted to play. They bet on his head, otherwise wanted nothing from him. They just wanted to play and bet on him: execution or not. New game, new luck. The music made everyone hungry and thirsty, and the fashionable gentlemen whistled in annoyance because they were not satisfied with his execution. Like a beggar he stood in front of a church portal. Did the people want to spit in his face, did they understand him, or did they want to crown him? He would have liked to roar, but he found no voice. His legs turned weak. So his father was sitting in a theater loge, at the side of his mother, who sat regally in her wheelchair, behind her his brother, whose hand lay protectively on Mother's shoulder, and he himself, he, the professor, he was standing on a large, bare stage and from a ramp telling his father about the grass. For a long time he told about it, with choice words, until applause swelled up, until his father nodded benevolently in his loge, until he raised his hand in agreement, and finally the heavy curtain fell between him and the applauding public. He had seen even his brother clapping, only Mother's hands lay quietly in her lap. Slowly he went down the steps, flashbulbs glimmered around him, the music died away, the applause faded. The ghosts had broken through the wall. Nothing could have held them back. The ghosts that he believed in he had long since banished. He waded through paper; it lay everywhere; ankle-high he waded. It rustled like leaves under his steps; it rustled like his childhood. From the garden came a heavy, sweet smell, a smell of palaces, art, and culture, of prosperity and power, also a smell of violence and corruption, of false promises and red plush armchairs, of walls on which hung wreaths and portraits of fame, a smell of manufacturers' villas, of riding equipment, compasses, surveying instruments, and construction plans for superhighway bridges.

In the middle of Macao it smelled like Thulsern. The hysterical merriness that came from the foyer of a large hotel alarmed him. He was startled by the candlelight and the lilac dress coats of the waiters whom he watched through the windows serving. He thought he could hear the clinking of sinfully expensive watches that coiled around the slender wrists of supple beauties. Then he wanted to throw his money onto the street and buy his freedom from a beggar, but his shame was not sufficient to take care of his European debt. Macao presented Europe with the check. He pressed between stools and chairs that were set up in front of a bar; his hand clenched a brass staff; his gaze was glassy eyed, and Macao streamed past, rich, elegant, miserable Macao, a whoring Macao, the Macao of arrogant Europeans and clever Asians, the Macao of curiosity, of desire, of failure. The girls showed their slit clothes, paraded like decorated circus nags, clipped and clapped on high European heels. Wordlessly he continued his way. The displays revealed their treasures under neon light; men were having their hair waved, were being rubbed down, sprinkled with colognes, but he saw himself kneeling in a confessional, the confessional of the pilgrimage church, St. Vitus, in Thulsern, that confessional in which he had for the first time smelled the aroma of the naked body of a girl; he wanted to confess: In humility and repentance I confess all my sins, *ego te absolvo*, said a voice, even before he had recited his list; he absolved himself. He saw the grating of the confessional window and smelled the red-wine-sour breath of Wolffenzacher, the prelate, with whom he had learned to confess, who had confirmed him. Wolffenzacher held a sermon for him, then he stood as though benumbed and sunken in thought. Once in a while he stuck out a hand without cause and touched one object or another. The feeling overcame him that his death would not be taken note of by one or another office and that he was being shoved back into life. Had he become a priest as his mother wanted, he would also hear confessions, hear about the petty misdeeds, about lascivious women tourists who had fucked the ski instructor.

    And suddenly he is seized by the mania to whet a scythe, no, to take an ax in his hand, a sharply ground ax to split wood. The wish strikes him like lightning. He would like to split heavy firewood logs, would like to drive the iron into them and hear the wood cracking dryly, would like to swing the logs high in the air with the ax, with both hands, over his head, and then let them fall on the chopping block, would like to have his hands sticky with resin, would like the ax to be an extension of his arm, and again up with all that, swung high over his head, and down on the block until the wood is split, split again with a heave, and again and again. The marvelous aroma of fresh wood was set free; he breathed it, inhaled it, sweating, the sweat would be running from his brow; the ax would lie heavily in his hand, and it would be lying peacefully. For entire days he sees himself felling trees, sees himself cutting branches off, peeling the bark, sawing up the trunk, first a foot, then a yard, piling up the boughs and hacking them into pieces; he feels the labor in his bones; he feels dog-tired by evening and yet very hale, with dirty fingernails and happily skinned hands and arms, and the next day he would accept the invitation to a hunt with two friends. They would start out early, very early, out to the fog-drenched clearings, in rough clothes, schnapps for stimulation, and then they would shoot at anything that moved, would boom around and kill, extricate later and fry and eat and drink until they could no more, would fall wearily onto the cots in a log cabin, from which smoke would be climbing, while outside the snow would fall, more and more snow, until the cabin would be snowed in as in a fairy tale, completely and totally snowed in; and he would again step before the house, again would chop wood with stiff hands—for it would have to be bitterly cold—for the bulky thundering stove, and he would turn into Jack London; and Alaska or Canada would be everywhere, wherever he might be. He would own a spry team of sled dogs that would pull him over broad expanses of frozen seas, lonesome, muffled, a small pack, and a rifle on top that would always hold a last bullet ready for him. It made him happy that in this snowy desolation, he wouldn't find a person with a backbone that was twisted in a grotesque way, as though a great force had tried to turn it into a spiral; he hastened his steps and dreamed his dream right into almond eyes that looked at him and then lowered their glance as though it were happening out of respect before one whom all saw was already in the clutches of death.

Poisonous fog enveloped him and slowly lightened. He stood like an executioner and was, after all, the delinquent. The street became narrow. It sank, and he tumbled over the execution square. He had to reach into the air to keep hold of himself. There were ruins; he was moving between ruins. The idea of his execution drove him; he wanted to be faster and yet was slower. His breath seemed no longer sufficient. A little more and he would vomit from pain.

He saw pictures of marathon runners, how they reached the stadium, how the crowd shouted for joy, how the runners did the last laps: another five hundred yards, another four hundred, another three hundred, another two hundred yards to the hotel.

The crowd was jubilant, spurred him on.

He ran until he plunged into the inordinately large Macao moon, which seemed to be waiting for him.

And then I struck.

I awoke in the arms of an old woman peeling potatoes.

She accompanied me to my room.

How long I slept, I no longer know.

Late in the evening or deep into the night he undresses and in surprise reads a sign that during his absence was fastened to the door to the bathroom: *out of order*. He must find the bathroom at the end of the long, terribly lighted corridor. At this thought he feels taken advantage of, for he imagines it stopped up and completely filthy, with pools of stinking urine. About every twenty yards weak violet lamps throw strips of light onto the frayed purple carpet.

It's like being in the movie theater.

Right in the middle of the corridor, too, there burns such a lamp, like an emergency light. To the right of the lamp is the stairs, to the left the glass double doors to the aforementioned place in question. I slip into my bathrobe and step into the empty corridor. At the bathroom I am standing in front of a man who likewise is wearing a bathrobe and obviously had come from the opposite direction. From the distant end of the hallway a mirror observes us secretly.

The man walks with a cane like a blind man and—I can't believe it, no, it can't be true—the man resembles: BORGES.

The way he holds the cane, the way he wears his double-breasted robe.

It *is* Borges.

So he exists after all.

But it can't possibly be he, for how would he have come here to this rundown Portuguese colonial structure, which with its crumbling façade and the steep, crooked balconies tells the fairy tale about the grand old days of sunken splendors. I did read in Rome about Borges' death: in black and white. I remember the headline exactly.

But it's Borges: the way I got acquainted with him in the Academy of Fine Arts, the way he stood in front of me in the flesh and signed my copy: *The Book of Imaginary Creatures*.

His eyebrows and lashes flutter briskly over his blind eyes, as though the eyelids in his face, like sails under his eyebrows, had become wings: The wings of his eyes, that he sends out like carrier pigeons, that he lets circle around the whole world in order, after their return, to have them report everything to him again and again, so that he will miss nothing new or old nor be discovered for illuminating concealment.

I can't just simply speak up and say:

There is no you, Borges, for all the newspapers reported about your death.

There never was a you, Borges, for Señor Christofari proved conclusively that you were a puzzlement.

I just can't do that.

But perhaps with his appearance he wants only to prove one of his famed sayings, according to which a man who has commerce with the dead forgets that he is a dead man.

He proves to me that all of creation is *one book,* in which all the mysteries of life are recorded, if we only understand how to read the book correctly.

No, he proves to me merely a single saying:
Little has happened to me, but I have read a lot.

We almost collided, and my opposite is astonished also and embarrassed and hesitates a moment. It is obviously uncomfortable for us both to walk ahead of one another through the mirrored door. So I just walk on. And what does he do? He does the same thing.

Mirror!

Again and again Borges wrote about mirrors.

Night and blindness were to him the mirrors of cognition, every book a mirror of the face that bent over it.

But most frightening of all is the mirror that waits for each man who has swallowed rat poison.

Even with my first step I am annoyed at my stupidity, but what should I do? There are only two possibilities: Either I walk to the end of the corridor and then turn around; and if I'm lucky, the man who resembles Borges to a T, the same stature, the same attitude of the head—the face is not recognizable in this dim light—so, if I'm lucky, then that man will have disappeared. But what if he too walks on in embarrassment and acts as I do? Then we'll bump into one another again without fail, and I'll stand there even more stupidly. Or—the second possibility—I hide in one of the deep doorways (they are dark enough), watch the corridor, and wait until it's all clear.

Ridiculous, this hide-and-seek. But even before I can grab that thought, I again crouch like a thief in a black niche.

The door has the number 48. Like the flight from Surabaya to Bandung.

What will happen, if suddenly the guest in 48 returns—or leaves his room? From my behavior he can draw only unmistakable conclusions. Even worse: Perhaps 48 is the very room of that man who resembles Borges in a devilish way. If he returns now, I'm trapped. I must leave my hiding place at once. The corridor is completely empty. No figure with a blind man's cane, no footfalls, no creaking of boards, nothing, only the violet light of the movie theater lamps. Painstakingly casually I walk toward my room.

Then my glance falls accidentally on a painting on the wall. Because of the mediocre lighting I cannot make out exactly what the picture depicts. All the more remarkable is the gleam of a small brass plate in the middle of the lower frame, on which I decipher the name *Christofari*.

And then I recognize something else in the dim light: Next to the large dark painting hang a few smaller pictures in little oval frames, arranged like a gallery of ancestors in the parlor of a bourgeois household. I know what is depicted in the small pictures; I know it without having to look.

It is the *Madonna col bambino* that my student-days colleague Herzig wanted to research. Mary always has the Baby Jesus on her arm, and the Baby Jesus has a songbird in his hand. And from picture to picture the faces of Mary become more peasantlike, coarser, uglier, and the Baby Jesuses become broader in the skull, hollower, more brutal and more monstrous until finally they grow into fat infants with maliciously petrified old men's faces. While in the first pictures they balance the little bird gracefully on the outstretched little fingers, from picture to picture the little patty-cake hands close more and more about the bird until finally it is squashed by loathsome sausage fingers. Unmercifully the Jesus monsters squeeze the throat of the bird. Hardly have I turned my gaze from the gleaming little brass plate when I see with horror how the double of the great Argentine is in the process of venturing at the other end of the hall out of a dark door recess, perhaps even from the niche to my room, and he already comes toward me with his cane. From the pocket of his jacket, as I can clearly see in spite of the dim light, peeps a wine bottle.

Again we meet right in front of the door to the bathroom; again neither dares to enter the bathroom before the other; again I am ashamed and know that my opposite is also ashamed.

I turn on my heel and walk straight to my room. Before I close the door, I quickly peer over my shoulder and see the other likewise standing at his room door staring over his shoulder at me. Softly I close the door, turn the key twice, strip off my bathrobe, throw it over the chair, and lie down on the bed.

My stomachache gets worse.

Is it the rat poison that is beginning to work?

Like a colic the cramps repeat. Sweat breaks out on my brow. I have to get out, else I can't stand it anymore.

Cautiously I open the door. Deep quiet lies over the violet hallway: yawning emptiness.

I race.

But, as on command, Borges is there again. As though mesmerized out of the floor, he, too, suddenly is running with great, elegant strides toward the redeeming door.

For the third time we are standing opposite one another in front of the milk-glass panes.

For the third time we are putting on this amateur show.

For the third time we avoid one another and cannot look one another in the eye.

Again I land with my cramps in the dark door niche of number 48. Without peering out, I know that

Borges likewise is hiding in one of the recesses, possibly the one to my own room. I decide to wait until the other one leaves his hiding place.

But my cramps become worse and worse.

A choking in my throat is added.

Why does the other one not dare to come out?

He just won't come out, as long as I don't come out.

The cramps are so strong that I fall on my knees.

Borges doesn't show himself.

The pains are superhuman.

I crouch in my niche, begin to whimper.

Finally he sees with strained, quickly weaker eyes how little by little more and more hotel guests leave their rooms, step out into the corridor to crouch in strange, dark door recesses. They are figures that he knows.

Almayer is among them with Nina, his beautiful daughter, Sancho Panza, Dulcinea, Don Quixote, and many others.

And all of them are well known to him. He recognizes them, there isn't the slightest doubt of that; he knows them exactly, for they have met him very often. They were the only company that he had put up with all his life, because he knew he could always blindly rely on them. They would never disappoint him.

Many of them slide softly to the floor; others collapse immediately; but most of them sleep standing like beasts of burden, as though they had long been under way in the quicksilvery half darkness.

Damned be the one who comes for my bones.

He was again Alonso Quijano, on his last ride, in his last dream, when he was dreaming of being Don Quixote.

Led by slack reins and unsure spurs, Rosinante returned to the village from which they had once set out; and she would have erred at every forking of the way, had she not had the help of her sole compass and magnet, the remembrance of her old stall.

Her amble unsteady, her tongue hanging and ears tired, her eyes cloudy, as though through a fog.

Any joyfulness seemed obliterated in the deeds of the man who had set out with the idea in his head of challenging the wind. For him all adventures were a single one.

But the boards on which he set his soles were rotten.

With nothing but this knowledge did he return.

No one at home, no one in his last chamber, in which he would lie down to die.

He felt relieved.

A bed at the window, through which a piece of sky came.

Under the linen cloth the old man laid his withered knees next to one another and looked toward that piece of sky, the clouds, and their hasty discord. And he imagined they were flowers or collapsing mountain ranges.

It is time to return home.

You have traveled so much.

I made seven journeys, and on each one hangs a wondrous story that can bewilder the mind.

You fought so much, but you never learned to lose.

There is only one way of being Don Quixote: You must set your ideals even higher.

Now you are only a souvenir.

Wake up from your dreams.

They were windmills, nothing more.

When he awoke, he knew that this was his death.

Before him comes forth the picture of all the life of mankind on earth, and that human life seems to him to be nothing but a tiny flicker in a boundless darkness.

His life, too, particularly his, was ridiculous and trifling, and with the last beat of his heart his defiant renunciation was to sound into the all-devouring darkness.

Epilogue

There was a smell of snow in the air, my love life was a mess, my work had become a mockery, my parents had died, my friends had turned away from me.

I was at the end of my rope. I locked the doors and windows and became absorbed so deeply in the world of books that my nights from twilight to dawn and my days from dawn to dusk passed while I was reading.

Only books remained.

Let others boast about the pages they have written; I am proud of those I have read.

Ten thousand books, and over each one hovers a ghost.

But in the end, finally, everything is reduced to

becoming ridiculous or at least pitiful, be it as grand and significant as it may. There is no other possibility than in the end to find everything ridiculous or at least pitiful.

Never has there been a more ridiculous figure than the knight of the woeful countenance.

And still, his shadow, which reaches over the centuries, is alone enough to transform the image of one scorned and piteous into a glowing model in which compassion endures like a fly in amber.